I Can Hear *the* Mourning Dove

I Can Hear *the* Mourning Dove

James Bennett

Houghton Mifflin Company
Boston   1990

Library of Congress Cataloging-in-Publication Data

Bennett, James W., 1942–

I can hear the mourning dove/James Bennett

p. cm.

Summary: Gifted but severely mentally disturbed, sixteen-year-old Grace moves back and forth between school and hospital, where she receives unexpected support from an antisocial delinquent named Luke.

ISBN 0–395–53623–5

[1. Mentally ill—Fiction.] I. Title.

PZ7.B43989Iab   1990   89–26680

[Fic]—dc20   CIP

AC

Printed in the United States of America

BP   10   9   8   7   6   5   4   3   2   1

*This book is dedicated to the memory of
Terrence Lore Smith, my best friend,
without whose help and encouragement
I never would have been a writer at all.*

One

ON THE DAYS when it's not terribly hot, Mrs. Higgins turns off the air-conditioning in the lounge and opens some of the windows. I like the breeze at the open window and I sit on the blue couch. That's when it's so peaceful, and if I listen very carefully, I can hear the mourning dove. The dove says:

Oooooo ooo ooo
Cooooo ooo ooo

The cooing is peaceful and reassuring. I am sitting in the sunken garden at Allerton under the warmest sun that ever was. An old science teacher bursts into my brain, very smug in his opinion that birds *never make any noise whatsoever unless they are threatened or stressed.* It would be hard to make a statement more false; but to learn the truth he would have to sit in the Allerton sun in a state of inner peace and listen to the mourning dove. I choose not to remember the teacher's name, and I would prefer him to keep his self-righteous ideas out of my brain altogether.

Oooooo ooo ooo
Cooooo ooo ooo

*

This is a different day. I'm quite sure about that. Of course, I could simply look at the logic of it: this is a day, and every day is different, so this has to be a different day. It is not the same day.

I don't always know what place this is. Mostly, I'm quite sure it's a hospital. There are colored lines of tape on the wall, down near the baseboard. There is a blue line, a red line, a green line, and a yellow line. Too many lines at once is too much data. It's not necessary for the tape to be fluorescent because they always leave the hall lights on, but I'm very fond of fluorescent tape. The lines are there in case you get scrambled, so you can find your destination.

There is no tape at Allerton, but there are always gravel paths to lead the way. The formal gardens have hedges that make diagonal rows and rectangular rows; there is so much geometry. It is blissful there, in the warm sun, and my father is a nourishment.

The hospital has lots of new wings, which are actually quite ugly. It has wings but it can't fly. This thought makes me giggle.

Mrs. Higgins says to me, "What's funny, dear?"

"It takes wings to fly, but they have to be the right wings."

"Grace, you need to get dressed. You're still in your nightgown."

If I know her name is Mrs. Higgins, then I must know what place this is. I say to her, "What place this is, I know not."

Mrs. Higgins has blurry edges because she's standing in the mist. People in the mist float a few inches off the ground since there's less gravity. There's some gravity, otherwise they would float high in the sky right on through the stratosphere and the atmosphere and the biosphere.

I ask Mrs. Higgins what day it is.

"It's Tuesday, dear."

"You're quite sure about that?"

"Yes, I'm sure. If you go and take a shower and get dressed,

2

you'll feel much better." After that, I don't know what she says. Her voice is quite electrical.

*

Some days I go flat out and the days crawl by and the nights go on forever. About all I do is sit and cry like a baby, and I wonder *what's the use*. Some nights the nightmares come.

My mother visits me and I'm so flat out I don't feel like talking.

"How's your appetite?" she wants to know. "Are you eating well?"

I shrug. "Who cares?"

"I care, and you'd better care."

I just shrug again.

She bores in. "What did you have for dinner last night?" She's very persistent.

I say to her, "We had breaded pork tenderloin, mashed potatoes with gravy, roll with butter, and strawberry Jell-O."

"I know you didn't eat the tenderloin; did you eat the potatoes?"

"Pork gravy on them. I ate some of the Jell-O."

"Have you told them you're vegetarian?"

"I've told them I'm a vegetable."

"I don't see the humor, Grace. If you don't tell them, I will."

"Please stop boring in. I get sick, sick, sick of telling them things." It grieves me the way I talk to my mother. She's so patient and I am such a cross for her to bear.

*

I wake up in the middle of the night and the freight train is roaring through my bedroom. I sit straight up in bed and hug my knees. The roar is so deafening it vibrates the room. I am trembling all over and drenched with sweat; my teeth are chattering.

3

In the other bed, Mrs. O'Rourke is sleeping soundly. The whole building is shaking and she sleeps. I dare not move a single inch to the right or left, or else I will be pulverized beneath the steel wheels of the locomotive. I see myself dismembered, and severed into scraps of flesh and bone.

Then there is screaming. I can hear it clearly. It even wakes Mrs. O'Rourke up. She slept through the train, but not the screaming. The screams are louder and louder and closer and closer and then I realize that they are my own. I am the one who is screaming.

Mrs. Grant comes in a hurry from the hallway. The two of us are sitting on the edge of the bed; she has her arm around my shoulders. It's hard for me to talk because I still have the shakes.

"Mrs. Grant, do you not hear the train?"

"There's no train, dear, it's just the nightmare."

"Be sure to sit still, Mrs. Grant, or the wheels of the train will crush us to bits."

This is how it started. Nightmares. Nightmares with bed-wetting — it's so humiliating.

"Not the train again? It's only a nightmare; everything is okay." She dabs the sweat from my forehead. My complexion is bad; my mom urges me to take better care of it, but I am neglectful. Thinking this wretched thought, I start to cry, and Mrs. Grant holds me again.

*

Dr. Phyllis Rowe asks me lots of questions about my father. She must think it's an important thread in the fabric of my make-up.

I am walking with my father in the field across the pond from the elegant Georgian mansion at Allerton. At the far end of the field there are woods. We always pick wildflowers as we go: violets, daisies, clover, and trillium. There are fuchsia bushes growing among the rocks at the edge of the woods; the bees are so thick the bushes seem to hum with a voice all their own. The sun is warm in the bluest blue sky.

"Tell me about picking wildflowers with your father."

"Sometimes we would find the wild roses that grow in the woods, the little tiny ones in bunches. He would cut me some with his pocket knife. They are tiny and white. He used to carry balls of yarn in the back pocket of his blue jeans; we used the yarn to make an *Ojo de Dios.*"

"What is *Ojo de Dios?*"

"It means God's Eye."

"Yes, but what is it?"

"It's a craft. You tie two sticks in the shape of a cross, then you cover the spaces with different colored yarn. You wrap the yarn in the shape of a diamond." *The eye belongs to the voice, and the voice to the eye. But I'd better not tell her that.*

"Your father was good at crafts."

"He was an artist. He was very good with his hands and very good with his heart. His hands were rough and brown, but they were tender and gentle. Sometimes I think Jesus Christ had hands like my father."

"That's a nice thought. You were very close to your father."

She insists on using the past tense. "We were very close."

Maybe there's an eye in the sky that rotates and pivots and searches into every secret, private corner in the universe. Maybe it's a merciless eye that knows your thoughts and can influence your thoughts. Maybe the eye uses the voice. But I don't think the eye could be an *Ojo.*

"Besides picking wildflowers and making God's Eyes, what did the two of you do together?"

"We did everything together. We walked the grounds of Allerton from one end to the other. We made things together. We read

5

together, especially poetry. I went with him on a peace march once — it was a protest of military force in Nicaragua. Sometimes after supper, he took me to the art room at the high school. He made a lovely sculpture of Beauty and the Beast out of junk and scraps. He could do things like that."

"Grace, you've never mentioned your friends to me."

"I don't have friends."

"If that's true, why is it true?"

I just know I'm going to get scrambled; she's going to cause it. I don't want it to happen, so I talk as fast as I can: "Our house was in the country, I rode the bus to school and I rode the bus home. Our neighbors didn't have children. Everything I just said is probably irrelevant; I wouldn't have had friends anyway. People scare me and I'm too weird. I am crazy wild this very moment."

"Sometimes it seems maybe your father was your best friend."

I stop talking because the tears are running down my face. *How did I get this way?* It's so lonely and miserable and degrading.

Dr. Phyllis Rowe has her hand on my hand and she's asking more questions. If she wants to know so much about my dad, why doesn't she let him answer for himself? Her voice is a storm of static.

She is receding down this incredibly long tunnel, like Alice floating through space. She is just a speck.

*

The razor blade I use for slitting my wrist is a single-edge blade with a rounded metal shield on one side. It belongs to my father. He has lots of them. Artists use them to scrape paint from glass and other hard, slick surfaces.

My plan is to cut both wrists, but when the blade slices the flesh it hurts a lot more than I expected. I am sitting in the bathtub,

6

squeezing the bleeding left wrist under the water, and for a moment I think only of the pain. The blood billows into the water like red cumulus clouds. The clouds toss and tumble in the water, shifting colors from deep rose to a shade so pale it is nearly pink.

I stretch out in the tub so that only my head and shoulders are above the water. I only know that a sense of purpose is very purifying. The hot water is still running from the tap; there is rising steam and crimson water. I feel pleasantly faint in a peaceful sort of twilight zone. They will find me naked, but it won't be embarrassing because I will be dead.

*

I wake up in the middle of the night with the shakes again. A siren is inside my head, trying to split my skull in two. The train is roaring. My nightgown is soaked with cold sweat; I lie in the fetal position and quiver. The train is shaking the whole earth. I am dizzy because I'm about to be tossed off the planet and into the abyss.

I make it to the bathroom, where I wipe my face and dab the towel at my stringy hair. It must have been a nightmare. I take off the soaked nightgown and I am standing naked in the harsh bathroom light. I have the shakes so bad I have to lean on the lavatory to keep my balance. I try some deep breathing. I look at myself in the mirror, my red watery eyes and my pasty white skin. I never shave under my arms. My mother says it's a tacky, sloppy thing, and if I shaved my armpits, and took care of my complexion, and did something with my hair, I would look better and feel better. I always shave my legs but it's absurd, really. I wear blue jeans every day so no one ever sees my legs but me.

I put on my robe and go to the lounge. When I pass the nurses' station, I don't look to the right or the left. The lounge is nearly empty because it's not yet dawn. I can only see two or three people,

7

and they are mostly floating in the mist. I sit on the blue couch beside the open window and hug my knees. The wind blows peace and quiet from the far-off university farm, cattle lowing and the rich smell of manure in a barn.

Even at this early hour, I can hear traffic noise from the interstate. The drivers are probably going to work. I'm sure they are very competent; they will drive their cars skillfully and arrive at their destinations on time. They will work in stressful offices all day without getting scrambled, and their personal relationships will be effective. Their lives are so good and so sound.

Dr. Phyllis Rowe is firmly convinced that my father is dead, but I don't have the energy to dispute with her. There's so much she doesn't understand. The Surly People run rampant in our new neighborhood. They trample underfoot whatsoever is good, whatsoever is kind, whatsoever is merciful, but how could I ever explain it to her? I've tried to tell her about the Surly People and I've tried to tell her about my dreams, but there's so much interpretation.

I know exactly what place this is. If my father comes today, he will be proud that I don't shave my armpits, that I haven't become a pawn in the empty game called the *Amerikan Way.* If he does come, I think I'll ask him if we can read some poetry.

"Grace, did you hear what I said?"

It's Mrs. Higgins. "Mrs. Higgins, I've meant to ask you. Why are there so many mirrors in the lounge?"

"It's used sometimes for aerobic and dance classes. Are you ready to get dressed?"

Mrs. Higgins is floating and misty. "Too many mirrors may not be a good thing, you know. They make so many facets. It can make a fractured person feel all the more fractured."

"I'll think that over."

Mrs. Higgins always means well, but her teeth are so long. I've

8

noticed it quite often in group therapy. Especially when she smiles: she's very long in the tooth. It seems to be the funniest thing I've ever heard, to be long in the tooth, and I start to giggle. I try to stop because I don't want to hurt her feelings, but that only makes it worse. Of course she doesn't know that I'm thinking about long in the tooth. I am laughing hysterically until the tears are running down my face.

*

"Momma is momma and poppa is poppa."

"What do you mean by that?"

"Momma does what momma does and poppa does what poppa does."

"Your father died in June of last year. You're not forgetting that, are you?" Her voice is popping and crackling with electrical charge.

She goes on. "Your mother and father had different values? Different goals and priorities? Is that what you mean?"

"That's it. Dr. Rowe, have I told you about the nightmares?"

"You've tried to from time to time. Are you still having the nightmares?"

"I always have them. I'm sure they must be important."

"If you want to be specific, I'll be happy to hear about them. If not, I'd rather not change the subject."

I'm starting to go flat out, but I say, "My dad was vegetarian. He thought it was barbaric to kill and devour a sentient being. I thought he was right. My mom didn't really go along with it. We ate different things at the dinner table. Sometimes my dad would fix some vegetarian thing for the two of us and Mom would have something else."

"Did they quarrel much about it?"

My mother is patient and kind; she has so much goodness. I say to Dr. Rowe, "They didn't quarrel much about anything. At least not in front of me. That's what I remember most: they weren't really together on things, but their antagonism was always below the surface. It wasn't out in the open." I'm flat out now, and I don't feel like talking.

"I'm listening," says Dr. Rowe.

I just shrug. At Allerton, the sun is warm, and the dove brings peace and harmony.

"Don't stonewall me," she says. "Please go on."

I shrug again. "Not worth the effort."

"*I* think it's worth the effort. You can give up on your own time if you want, but not on my time."

She ties my stomach in knots. "I've been trying to tell you."

"So keep trying. Your affect is completely flat." There is electrical interference in her voice. I don't know if it's charge or *dis*-charge. She tells me I have no affect. I have no effect either. If I died in the bathtub, no one would ever notice my absence.

"Dr. Rowe, I have no affect and no effect. Hospital language is crazy, it's crazy language for crazy people. Have you ever noticed that?"

"We were talking about your parents, Grace."

"I've been trying to tell you!" I snap. "My father felt things very deeply, and he was always full of energy. There was always a wrong to be righted."

"Such as?"

"Peace march, vegetarianism, animal rights. When my dad and I were together, we were always doing something or going somewhere."

"And your mother?"

"The opposite." She ties me up in knots the way she bores in.

10

She's boring and she's boring. She's asking me more questions but the only thing coming out of her mouth is electrical static.

*

This is the night that crawls by. Seconds are minutes and minutes are hours and hours are days. I can't go to sleep no matter how hard I try. I should ask for more medicine but I know they won't let me have it. Every scary thing that ever was makes a fiery chain in my brain. A nuclear war is incinerating the whole planet. I see burning streets and melting people, their flesh dripping from their bones like candle wax. In slaughterhouses poor beasts are getting butchered. They bleat out their panic and squeal out their terror and the blood gets washed away with a hose. I cover my ears with such pressure that my head begins to ache.

I get out of my bed and sit on the floor in the corner of the room and hug my knees. I pray for daylight. Why should my life be like this? If I shut out the frightening things in my own life, then the calamities of the whole earth take their place. I begin to sob, but at first I try not to make a lot of noise and wake Mrs. O'Rourke.

Now I'm crying so loud I wonder why she doesn't wake up. No nurse comes, so it must be that they can't hear me at the nurses' station. Mrs. O'Rourke is in for acute depression due to menopause; she will get better, everybody says so. I will never get better. The meaningful part of my life is over, if I ever had one. I'm sixteen now, if I live to be 80, that means 64 years of fear and getting scrambled. It's so obvious that the answer is death. Maybe my father will bring me one of his razor blades, but if he does I can't botch it this time.

Before dawn, I put on my robe. I go to the lounge and sit on the blue couch. A nurse I don't know follows me through the mist. She is asking questions, but I turn away from her and cover my ears.

11

She makes electricity. Then she leaves; she's probably going to get Mrs. Grant.

I am really scrambled. I hug my knees to try and stop the shaking. If Mrs. Hernandez comes, it means Dr. Barber is going to give me a jolt. They will take me to the treatment room and I will have to lie on the cold sheet. They will put the lotion and the electrodes on my forehead, and the rubber mouthpiece between my teeth. They will drip anesthetic into my veins. After I am unconscious, Dr. Barber will zap my brain with electric current. They will watch me flop around in a seizure. I will be like a flopping fish on a dock.

If Mrs. Hernandez comes, she will ask me if I have *voided,* or if I have *evacuated.* Hospital language is crazy language for crazy people. If I *void,* does that mean I vanish? Do I disappear as if the hand of God came down with a giant eraser and wiped me off the blackboard?

This thinking gives me the giggles, so now I have the shakes and the giggles at the same time. Thank God my mother can't see me.

*

8/18

Dear Diary:

The hospital is a warm, safe place but there's nothing of my father here. I need something of his. I would like Mother to bring Uncle Larry's fatigue jacket so I can wear it in group. It isn't really something of Father's, but he and Uncle Larry were so close. I would love to have my Beauty and the Beast statue, but it wouldn't do to have it here; someone might steal it or damage it.

Sometimes I have to suffer the voice. The voice comes of its own accord, like a whisper or a hiss. How is it that the voice knows my thoughts and gives me advice? The voice frightens me. I'm afraid

12

that the voice belongs to the eye, and the eye rotates in the heavens so it has total vision.

I have to stop writing. I get such a head rush when I try and think about the voice, lights are popping in my head like tiny flashbulbs.

Mrs. Grant is beside me with my medicine. She has cleansed herself of the mist. I take my pills and ask her to look at what I've written.

She says, "I think this is exactly what Dr. Rowe wants you to do."

"But I know nothing about writing a journal, I've never done it before. This material isn't organized or developed."

"It doesn't need to be," she says. "Dr. Rowe just wants you to write your thoughts and feelings. It's not homework for English class."

"Don't forget, Mrs. Grant, that English is my best subject."

She has a warm smile. I believe she is a dear and resourceful person. "Do you want to write some more, or would you like to take a walk?"

"I would enjoy taking a walk, but please do keep the static out of your voice."

We are in the south hallway. The yellow line and the red line are irrelevant; it is the green line which leads to the exit which leads to the lawn. I remind Mrs. Grant of this.

"We'll follow the green line all the way, Grace."

"There are so many lines, sometimes it makes too much data. You have to concentrate very hard on the one which applies to you."

"We may not need the tape at all, Grace."

It's a bold thought, but I fasten my eyes on the green line all the same.

The sun is warm on the lawn. I can hear the traffic noise from the highway, but I can't hear the cattle. There are no clouds; it's such a relief — the voice usually comes with the clouds. If there's

13

motion in the sky, you need the clouds to see it. At Allerton, the statue of the dying centaur is deep in the woods, far from the formal gardens. You can get there on a straight path lined by tall trees. The centaur is huge and dying, dying lonely in the woods. But his death is heroic and magnificent.

I tell Mrs. Grant how death can be misunderstood, but she says, "It depends on what you mean."

"When the centaur dies and the leaves fall it is beautiful."

"Leaves are beautiful when they die, but why are we talking about death?"

The sun is warm, but I can't hear the cattle. I have a knot forming in my stomach. "Mrs. Grant, if I'm going to keep a journal, should I start out every page with *dear diary?*"

"If you want to, why not?"

"It seems so childish. Girls who write *dear diary* write about parties and proms and boyfriends." I wish I could hear the cattle, but of course: this is midday, it's not milking time. If my mind is this clear, I will be in control again soon. I'm getting short of breath.

"Mrs. Grant, I have to be sure about the date. If I'm going to keep a diary, I have to have accurate dates."

"Today is Monday, the eighteenth."

"That's what I wrote down, but I have to be sure. I get so confused about dates."

"You can be sure; this is the eighteenth." She smiles.

"It seems personal though, doesn't it, Mrs. Grant? Writing a diary and beginning each page with a greeting?"

"Yes, it does."

My teeth are chattering. "I think we should go back inside now."

"So soon? We've only been here a few minutes, Grace."

"Yes please. Let's go back inside now."

14

"Okay. Would you like to listen to your tape?"

Her voice is full of static. She means well, but it's something she can't control.

*

"I've told you before, Grace; no ECT."

"Dr. Barber gives me shocks."

"Dr. Barber *gave* you shocks. This is a different hospital, and I'm not Dr. Barber."

"Is Mrs. Hernandez coming?"

"Who is Mrs. Hernandez?"

"She's the nurse who gets me ready when I'm going to get jolted."

"Try to listen to what I'm telling you. This is a different hospital. We don't give shock therapy to teenagers."

"But the part you don't understand is that I'm really sick now. I used to be depressed, but now I'm schizo."

Dr. Phyllis Rowe is looking through my folder. She lights a cigarette. She blows out some smoke in streams through her nostrils. She frowns and says, "You've never been diagnosed schizophrenic."

"I know, but I'm sicker now. Before, I had depression. That was when I cut myself."

"Do you feel the urge to cut yourself now?"

"No. Not too often, I mean. Once or twice. Last night, I think it was. Can you give me something to help me sleep?"

"Yes. I'll see that you get something. What makes you think you're schizophrenic?"

"I know about schizophrenia. I've read about it and I've listened to other patients."

"But why do you think it applies to you?" She blows out some smoke and crosses her other leg.

"I hear my father's voice and I hear the sky whispering."

15

"Go on."

"I know he's dead, but he speaks to me. He *tries* to speak to me. I don't know if I should listen. There's something important he's trying to say to me."

"What is the important thing?"

"The voice gives me warnings. I must be vigilant and ever alert with respect to the Surly People. There is much more than meets the eye. *Semper Fidelis.*"

"Grace, who are the Surly People?"

"I've told you about them before. I'm not sure if the voice is actually speaking to me or if I just hear it in my head. Sometimes I think the thoughts are my own thoughts, but in his voice."

"Your father's voice?"

"Yes."

"What about the whispering?"

"The whispering comes from the sky, when the clouds get blown around. If the clouds move fast, the whispering gets louder."

"What does the whispering say?"

What if the voice belongs to the eye? Should I ask her about that? I say, "I don't know. It's like whispering in a library, I can't make out the words." I feel tears coming to my eyes, and a lump in my throat. I say to Dr. Rowe, "I'm really scared. If I'm schizo, then I'm not going to get any better."

"Nonsense. If this is a schizophrenic process, then it's reactive and sudden, which means your chances for recovery are good." For the first time, her voice is starting to crackle and pop with electrical static, but I really don't want to get scrambled, I need her to help me. She goes on. "I don't like labels much, and this one scares you, so why don't we just say that you're going through something acute, and you need to get better?"

"Tell me I'm not schizo. Please."

She is stubbing out her cigarette and shaking her head. "I'm not

16

prepared to deny it or confirm it. Would it do you any good to have the label? In any case, we still don't give ECT to teenagers."

Her voice is crackling with static. Like a shorted radio, some of her words are loud and clear and others I can't even hear. I'm starting to tremble, and hoping she can't see it. I'm taking deep, deep breaths so as not to get scrambled, but I am losing it.

*

I have a nightmare about the train. I sit up straight in bed with the shakes. It's five A.M. The bathtub was so very white, it was either porcelain or enamel. The blood runs down the drain, that must be where it goes. After the drain, I'm not sure how far the blood runs; it may be only a few feet, or it may be clear to the core of the earth.

I put on my robe and hurry to the lounge. There's no daylight yet. I curl up against the back of the couch and pull my robe up tight under my chin.

Mrs. Grant comes, floating close with her blurry edges.

"Please don't disturb me," I say. "I've got the shakes."

If Mrs. Hernandez comes, they will put me on the table and strap me down and wire me. I hope and pray she doesn't come.

"I'm scrambled, Mrs. Grant."

"It's going to be okay, Grace. I'll sit with you." She is holding my hand.

"Be sure and anchor yourself," I remind her. "Your gravitational field is not strong."

The room is so misty. In the corner, Miss Ivey is sitting in front of the television set. The set is on, but there is only a bluish test pattern and a high-pitched hum. There isn't much to Miss Ivey except skin and bone. She has disheveled white hair and she's wearing a gray flannel nightgown. Her left hand is holding her right wrist; her right hand is vibrating in front of her face. I can't tell if the hand holding the wrist is causing the shaking, or slowing it down.

17

"In a little while you will be getting your medication," says Mrs. Grant.

The high-pitched hum from the test pattern is making my eyes ache. I wish I had the courage to turn the set off, but I wouldn't dare; there's no telling what Miss Ivey might do. Miss Ivey is a crone, I decide. I love archaic words. Suddenly, the word *crone* seems to me the funniest thing I've ever heard of. I am laughing so hard I've got tears and little convulsions. I want to say to Mrs. Grant, *Miss Ivey is a crone,* but I'm laughing too hard to speak, and if I try to stop it only gets worse.

Mrs. Grant is patting me on the shoulder and brushing the hair out of my eyes. The test pattern is carving in my brain like a probe; my skull is splitting open like a stone. I am out of control altogether. The laughter has turned to crying. I'm sobbing myself out but Mrs. Grant has her arm around me.

Two

"**I** AM CONDEMNED." My words are monotone words, like I'm not even the one speaking them. No affect. "Condemned to freedom."

"You sound like a prisoner."

"Of course, a prisoner. Is it any use to pretend something else? It is a lifetime sentence which can't be suspended. No time off for good behavior, and no chance for parole."

"Such a gloomy picture you paint. You wouldn't rather stay in the hospital, would you?"

"Yes. Maybe. I'm not sure. What difference does it make? When you're wacko, your sentence goes whither thou goest. You could give me a lobotomy. I would have a tell-tale scar across my forehead like Frankenstein's monster, but I would be a rock. I would be level every day. I would be so level I could make God's Eyes every day and you could sell them in the hospital gift shop."

Dr. Rowe lights one of her cigarettes and smiles at me. "I'll take that under advisement," she says.

She turns to my mother. "You and Grace have many new things in your lives," she says.

Mother is sitting straight in her chair. Her hands are folded in her lap. "Maybe too many," she says.

"Maybe too many indeed. A new city, a new job for you, and a new school for Grace. That's a lot of change to deal with."

My mother laughs nervously. "I know," she says. "Do you have to remind me?"

Dr. Rowe smiles again. "Among other things," she says, "we've been trying to remind Grace that *anyone* face-to-face with this much change would feel a great deal of stress."

I just can't believe it. She thinks I've been talking about stress. My stomach cranks into a knot that fills up my whole abdomen. How could she understand? In her experience, feelings are cause and effect; or is it cause and affect? How could I make her understand? What words are there that could make either one of them understand? I feel tears stinging my eyes.

"Mother will handle it," I mumble. "She's a rock and she will handle it."

"You don't really believe your mother is a rock."

"Of course I do. Of course I don't. Who cares, I can't say the things that matter, not with my brain whizzed up, when I can't think one thought after the other. When I'm not scrambled, I know my mother has feelings that other people have. But down here, in my stomach, it's like she's a rock."

"Mrs. Braun, is this something the two of you talk about?"

"We've talked about it. I think Grace believes I'm always in control. It's true I don't get hysterical about things, but I still have the same feelings that other people have. I feel a lot of stress about starting a career, but I don't lose sleep over it."

"You hear your mother, Grace; is that how you see it?"

"My mother talks like these things are choices, but she always speaks the truth."

"You don't believe that feelings are choices."

"How can I?"

"You believe that your mother will be able to handle the stress of all these changes, and you won't."

"It's true," I mumble. I do wish she'd stop talking about stress and choices; she's missing the point. I'd give anything to be like

20

my mother. She's not very exciting but she's *in control.* One foot in front of the other, one step at a time, one day at a time, a life without fear, without panic, without getting scrambled. Her life is so sound. She knows; I've told her so.

Then all of a sudden with no warning at all, the tears are running down my face. I can't help it, I can't stop the sobs. "The Surly People are there! They ruin everything! They have no regard for things that are lovely or beautiful!"

Mother scoots her chair next to mine and puts her arm around me. I'm still sobbing. She gives me Kleenex from her purse. I'm an albatross. I'm a huge parasite sucking her blood. You are always so pale, Momma, because I take your blood.

"I don't understand about the Surly People," says Dr. Rowe. "What does it mean?"

Mother answers. "She's talking about our new apartment complex. I have to admit it's pretty slummy, but it's what we can afford. There are a lot of hoodlums living there; at least that's what we called them when I was in school."

"These are the Surly People," says Dr. Rowe. "Are they teenagers?"

"Some of them are, and some of them are a little older, old enough to be living on their own. Quite a few of them don't actually live in our complex, they just seem to hang out there. We've only been there since the middle of July, but I think all of Grace's impressions are based on these hoodlums."

I'm blowing my nose. "My impressions aren't based on anything. I can't seem to get that point across."

Dr. Rowe corrects me politely: "What you mean is, not based on anything you can identify. Anyway, if you've only known these people for a month or so, why not keep an open mind? You can't always judge a book by its cover."

21

I look up and she is smiling at me. "Thank you for the cliché," I say. "But I don't know them, I only observe them. I wouldn't want to know them." I don't want to say any more; I feel myself going flat out.

The conversation turns to the terms of my discharge. Mother asks if it's the best time for me to be released.

Dr. Rowe says, "I'll tell you exactly what I've said to Grace; I'll give you a qualified *yes*. Her medication is helping, and both of us see improvement. Don't we, Grace?"

She is looking at me. I nod my head; it's so hard to get anything past her.

She goes on. "If this were the middle of the summer, I'd probably like to have her stay a little longer. But she's already being held back a year at school, so I think it's important for her to be there. Right from the first day, learning the ropes and making friends."

I've tried to tell her I don't make friends, but she ignores me.

Dr. Rowe says, "I've thought about keeping Grace here as a resident patient for another week or so, and having her schoolwork brought to the hospital. That's another option we have for adolescents, and we sometimes use it. But in my opinion, if she can be in her new school from the very first day, her chances of succeeding there will be better."

"But wouldn't it be better for her to get well first?"

Dr. Rowe smiles. Her cigarette is out. "If we talk about well, we have to talk about sick. I'd much rather talk about having problems and getting better. I'm not trying to pull rank on you; I've tried to say this is partly just a matter of timing."

Mother nods her head and bites her lip. "It might be easier for her than trying to start in a new school when she's already behind."

"I think so. Grace has so much hospital time in the last year that she's missed enough school to be out of sequence. If she can see herself getting better and succeeding in the real world, that's worth more than the hospital setting can provide."

Mother still seems uncomfortable. Maybe Dr. Rowe intimidates her, the way my father always did. "It's confusing," she tells Dr. Rowe. "I want to do what's best for Grace, but I never seem to know what best is."

"No one does for sure," says Dr. Rowe. "I'm giving you my best recommendation, but that's all it is."

Mother nods and Dr. Rowe goes on. "But just to give ourselves the benefit of both worlds, let's set up the best possible support system. We have an adolescent group that meets Monday and Wednesday evenings in the hospital annex. I'd like for Grace to be a member of that group, if you're both agreeable."

"That sounds good. What do you think, Grace?"

"It's okay." It's just fine with me if they go on talking and leave me out of it.

Dr. Rowe can tell. She speaks to me sharply. "Don't stonewall us, Grace. We've only got about five minutes left, and this is important."

"Okay, I'm listening."

"You must take your medicine every day, and on time. I want to see you in a week so we can monitor the medication again."

There is static in her voice, and I still have the knot in my stomach. "I'm listening," I mumble.

"The medicine will help, your mother will help, the hospital will help, and I will help. Even so, most of the help will come from you; you can be in control."

She means what she says, but it comes through her static.

She says to my mother, "We'll get Grace set up in the group and we'll call you for follow-up. You'll be hearing from us in a day or two."

23

We all shake hands and leave. It's hot in the parking lot with a blinding sun. There is haze. I have my suitcase in one hand and my overnight case in the other hand and I fix my gaze on my toes.

In the car, it's baking like an oven and the seat is hot as fire. I sit next to the door and hug my knees.

*

My secret, private nickname for the man in the next apartment is *Mr. Stereo.* Of course I would never call him that to his face or even speak to him. He is a huge man with powerful arms who could snap your neck like a twig.

He has many friends in his apartment late at night and they play the loud stereo, sometimes till two or three in the morning. It's mostly the bass that comes booming through the walls, as if someone were pounding on the walls with a muffled sledge hammer. It terrifies me. In the daytime, he sits out on his patio with his friend, where the two of them drink beer and play the loud stereo. They throw their cans on the ground. One of the speakers is next to them on the patio and the other is inside the apartment, but they leave their back door open. They are only six feet from our back door; a strip of gravel three feet wide separates his patio from ours, but there is no fence. It would help if we could close our windows but we don't have enough money to run the air-conditioning.

My mother has complained to the landlord and she has even complained once or twice to Mr. Stereo right to his face. He ignores her, but her courage astonishes me.

I could never find the words to describe how repulsive this row of complexes is. My father could, but he is dead. He would hate this place.

Suddenly, the sky says, *Try. Try and find the words.*

I have made a niche for myself on the second-floor balcony, just outside my bedroom. I sit on a wrought-iron chair in the corner, up against the bricks, in the shadow of the eave. I drape blankets and beach towels over the railing. I am safe and out of view, but there are slits for me to look through.

The sky comes on little cat feet. *Try. You are not alone. The words will come to you.* The sky is on fast-forward; the clouds are blown around, faster and faster, like the satellite pictures on the 10:30 news.

The sky whispers in my father's voice: *Try.*

But why?

Try. It's important. The voice urges me on.

I know the reason — the essence of the Surly People has to be identified and isolated. But *how* do I know this? Whence cometh this information? I have my diary and I will try to write it. It is my hand holding the pencil and moving it across the tablet, but who moves the hand? Who tells it what to write?

8/28

Dear Diary:

14th Street is a dead-end street, three blocks long. On our side of the street are twelve identical, plain, rectangular brick apartment buildings. There are four buildings per block. The buildings do not face the street; they face each other, across blacktop parking lots. Mother and I are in the apartment closest to the street, in the sixth building. We are one and a half blocks from MacArthur Street, where 14th Street begins.

I read what my hand has written, and it is nothing but dull information. It tells nothing of the noise or the filth or the trash or the sordidness or the ugliness or the way the Surly People trample on life.

I start to cry. I hate it when I cry all the time, but does the sky think that mere facts will somehow come to grips with the essence of Surly People, the way that psychiatrists think a long enough list of symptoms will cure a mental illness?

25

There's no answer from the sky. In fact, the sky is all gone now; no motion and no whispering. Maybe the whispering is just my father's voice in my own head; maybe that's all it ever is and there's no reason to be scared.

My mother wants to know why I'm crying.

I tell her I don't know. I want her to love me, but I'm not worth it. I want to be left alone.

"We ought to be going to the high school," she says.

"I'd rather stay home. Can't you take care of it?"

"I can't register for you, you have to be there. You've been flat out for two or three days. You need to snap out of it."

I don't say anything.

"Come on, get cleaned up a little bit. I'll be downstairs."

I wash my face a few times to get the red out, and pull the comb lazily through my clumpy hair. There is a crack in our medicine chest mirror, running almost straight from the upper left hand corner to the lower right.

In the kitchen, Mother wants me to eat something.

"Please, I'm not hungry."

"Dr. Rowe says you're less than a hundred ten pounds now."

"Don't worry, Mother, I may be crazy wild, but I'm not anorexic."

"That's not funny. I want you to have a little something. The least you could do is drink some orange juice."

I drink half a glass of orange juice and there is a sweet, nauseating lump in my stomach. I glance through the kitchen window; there are beer cans littered around Mr. Stereo's patio, but he is not outside yet. It must be too early in the morning for him. He never seems to go to work, where does he get his money for the beer and the stereo? Could it be that Surly People are sustained by some energy force all their own, and they don't need money?

We are in the car and on our way out of the parking lot. There is a narrow strip of grass between the end of each apartment building and the curb. I suppose they're called lawns but they are pitiful. At our house, when my dad was alive, we had a huge lawn and acres of fields and woods to walk in. The dairy farm was nearby and I loved the sounds and smells of the cattle.

The buildings here are probably no more than five years old. They only look this way because of neglect. This is a young slum. In Dickens stories, there are old slums. At least an old slum has character.

We are at the stop sign at MacArthur. There is an IGA grocery store on the corner and a huge parking lot. The parking lot is a congregating place for greasers and Surly People.

We cross MacArthur and it is six blocks on Roosevelt to the high school. The houses on Roosevelt are quite nice.

The high school is new and very big. There is a huge parking lot and lots of athletic fields. The halls are confusing to me, there is no tape here, but my mother helps me find the right office. We sit in the office of Miss Shapiro, who is a guidance counselor. Miss Shapiro is very young and she wears a great deal of bright red lipstick.

I am still flat out. My mother does most of the talking, which she doesn't like to do, but she probably figures we shouldn't take up too much of Miss Shapiro's time.

I am repeating the tenth grade; that's the first thing they talk about. This leads to a brief discussion of my mental history and my periods of hospitalization.

"Really?" says Miss Shapiro. She folds her hands on her desk and turns to me. "What seems to be the problem, Grace?"

What does she expect me to do with this question? She asks it the way she might ask someone for a sloppy joe recipe. I have had every test known to man, psychoanalysis, and a couple of ECT series. What kind of an answer does she expect from me?

27

"Excuse me," I say, "but there is static in your voice."

"What did you say?"

I feel humiliated. "The static. Can you not hear it?"

She looks very uncomfortable, and turns back to my mother. I have this sudden thought, that if I rolled my eyes or stuck out my tongue at her, Miss Shapiro would be scared to death. I almost giggle, but I don't.

Miss Shapiro asks my mother the same question.

My mother says, "Grace has been a resident patient and she's going to be receiving outpatient treatment. If you'd like to know more about it, maybe some other time."

"Of course."

"Could we please finish the registration now?"

"Of course." Miss Shapiro has forms on her desk. She asks questions and writes down the answers. I answer some of the questions about medicine, but Mother answers most of the others.

"And how about Grace's father?" asks Miss Shapiro. Her pen is poised.

"Deceased," says my mother.

Miss Shapiro says, "Diseased? He is diseased?"

"Not diseased," says my mother. *"Deceased.* He's dead."

My giggling is starting, and I can't control it. I am flushed all over. It's the tension, but I hate it when I get this way. "Mother, he's deceased because he was diseased." I'm out of control now.

My mother holds my hand. "Try a few deep breaths, Grace."

I can't even *catch* my breath. I'm laughing out of control, trying to bury my face. Miss Shapiro is staring at me with round eyes. I can't stop myself and there are tears rolling down my cheeks.

*

Wednesday is the first day of school. I feel better, I think maybe the medicine is helping me. Mother and I both leave the apartment at

28

7:30 A.M. I really wouldn't have to leave till eight, but I want to get past the IGA parking lot before the Surly People start to gather.

I am very scared at school, but I keep myself out of the flow. I follow the halls as best I can. I stay close to the walls. Every room is numbered, I'm sure I can learn to use the numbers. I try to get to each class early so I can sit in the back and not have to enter a room after it's full of other students. Most of the time is taken up with busy work and red tape; there are textbook rentals and other forms to fill out.

The cafeteria is full of people who know where to go and what to do. I look, and my ears pound; how would I ever find my way? Would there be anyone who would like me, or want to sit with me? I would get scrambled, then everyone would know. The panic is in me and the blood is pounding in my temples. Mr. Greene saves me: he says I can eat my lunch in homeroom because he is grading pretests. I sit in the back of the room and open the container of peach halves which my mother has packed for me. I nibble a few bits and drink some of the thick, sweet nectar.

Right after lunch is biology. The teacher, Miss Braverman, seems very nice, but there is the smell of formaldehyde. I hope we won't be cutting open some poor creatures.

My lab partner is a girl named DeeDee. She is attractive and poised; she seems friendly. She's probably a cheerleader and honor student. I ask her about dissection and she says, "I don't think there's any dissecting until second semester." The end of her answer pops with static.

Miss Braverman is talking about the science fair, but I don't know what that means. Besides, her voice has so much static all of a sudden and I feel myself getting lightheaded. The formaldehyde smell. On the shelves I can see rows of frogs suspended in little jars of clear liquid.

Oh God no, please not now, not here. I try deep breaths but it

29

isn't working; I don't trust my legs to try and leave the room. A gleaming scalpel blade slicing into the pale, white stomach of a pitiful frog. If only I didn't smell that smell.

I must be slumping down; the girl named DeeDee asks, "Are you okay?" That's the last thing I hear. The mist comes just before the darkness.

When I come to, I'm on a cot in the office of the school nurse. I know lots of nurses, but not this one; she seems pleasant enough, even though she's blurry in the mist.

"I got scrambled," I tell her. "Can you tell me the time, please?"

"It's almost three o'clock," she says. "Are you feeling better?"

"I guess so." She has a folder open. I can see the counselor, Miss Shapiro, in the doorway. She's blurry too, but I recognize her. I wonder if the two of them have been reviewing my psycho history.

"I called your mother," says the nurse. "She's going to pick you up in a little while."

"Thank you very much."

By the time Mother comes, I feel spent. We drive most of the way home without speaking. When she parks the car behind our apartment she says, "Don't get discouraged, we'll just take it one day at a time. Tomorrow will be better."

*

After supper, in my room. On my desk is the metal sculpture which my father made. It is Beauty and the Beast, welded out of metal scraps such as hinges, nuts, bolts, and washers. It is about eighteen inches high. Beauty has a nice shiny finish of bronze spray paint, but not Beast. I somehow feel sorry for his plain old rust. It might be that my dad meant to spray paint the entire statue, but I'm not sure. I put the statue on my lap and hold my arms around it. The sharp edge of the Beast's hinge cowl is cold against my cheek and there are tiny granules of rust which come loose and stick

30

on my skin. It was wonderful the way my dad could take trash or scraps and turn them into something lovely. The Surly People are just the opposite, they take whatsoever is lovely and defile it.

You need to get started on the letters.

When the voice comes so suddenly, it scares me. I open the file box in front of me. There is an old photograph of my dad and Uncle Larry when they were remodeling the kitchen in the stone house. Their shirts are off and their arms are around each other's shoulders. Uncle Larry was killed in action in Vietnam. He died before I was born, but I have his fatigue jacket and I wear it nearly all the time. I look at the photograph and my dad is dead too. My eyes fill up with tears; I have to write the Pentagon.

It's important to get started.

I am in control of my breathing. I wonder if Miss Braverman likes art; I wonder if I could ever be her friend. It's an absurd thought, really; why would a teacher want one of her students for a friend? Especially me. But I can tell she's very strong; it would be comforting to have a strong friend.

Don't let yourself get distracted. You have to get the letters written.

The voice scares me and energizes me. I write to Nieman-Marcus. I tell them never to buy or sell furs. I tell them that every fur represents real suffering. I send them a brochure on the cruelty of speciesism, printed by the *People for Ethical Treatment of Animals.* The second letter I write is to Congressman Stonecipher. I tell him about cruelty to laboratory animals and urge him to fight for animal rights. I send him a brochure too.

With no warning, the stereo starts.

My breath catches in my throat and I freeze. My clock says it's half past midnight. Oh no, I have to write the other letter.

Just as long as I don't panic. I start the letter, Dear Pentagon, but I don't know the name of a general. There should be a general's name, it can't be just Dear Pentagon.

31

The bass is booming through the walls. If the walls should crack, then what? The stereo is louder and louder. I can't let myself get scrambled, not again in the same day.

I wrap a pillow around my head to cover my ears. Dear Pentagon, I want to make certain my Uncle Larry's name is on the Vietnam Memorial. If someone could please check. There are so many names, one person could be overlooked.

The bass is louder and louder. My room is starting to shake. His name was Braun. You could look under the Bs. If only someone could please check.

"Mother! Can't you do something?"

I crawl onto my bed and hold the pillow tight around my head. I squeeze myself into a ball. "Mother!"

My mother comes and sits beside me.

"Can you hear it?"

"Of course I can hear it. I've already called the landlord." She is getting misty, with static in her voice. I can't get scrambled again in the same day, that didn't even happen in the hospital.

"Mother, I can't hear."

"It's going to be okay," she says.

I am shaking and shivering in my fetal ball. She wipes my forehead and pushes the strands of damp hair out of my face. Am I going to live my whole life like this? It's a desperate thought, no life at all is better than living like this. But I'm scared of dying too.

Sometime, I don't know when, the stereo goes off.

*

On Thursday and Friday it goes better, but I really hate P.E. We have to change into blue nylon Speedo swimsuits in the locker room. I don't like being naked in the presence of these people I don't even know. I was naked when I cut myself. I'm vulnerable

32

enough with my clothes on. I never wear a bra. My breasts are small and pointy, my underarms aren't shaved, my skin is too white, my complexion is bad, and my hair is clumpy; why should these girls know what I wear or don't wear, or where I shave or don't shave? I choose a locker in the corner and change as quickly as I can, all hunched over.

It's especially embarrassing in biology class, so I mostly keep my eyes down. Miss Braverman speaks politely to me, and my stylish lab partner asks me if I'm okay.

I mumble something, I'm not sure what. I take copious notes of everything Miss Braverman says, even though she's mostly just summarizing the class outline, which is printed on a handout.

*

Mr. Stereo has a new dog. He is a lovely little Doberman pup but his tail and ears are bobbed. His poor tail stump and his ear stumps are wrapped with adhesive tape. It is cruel and unusual punishment and completely unnatural. No animal should be mutilated just to satisfy some human's sense of style. The poor pup even has a large cardboard disc around his neck to keep him from biting at his tail. I wish Mr. Stereo didn't have the dog at all; he is ruthless, why should he have the right to own one?

My mother wants to take me to the mall so I can buy some new school clothes.

"It's too late, Mother; school already started."

"Please, Grace, let's just go."

I'm not enthused, but she has been nagging me for two days, and I agree to go. On the way, we stop at a supermarket. I remind my mother to buy some cans of applesauce and irregular peach chunks in heavy syrup.

When we get to Sears, she wants to buy me a racerback bra. They're on sale.

"Mother, you know I never wear a bra."

"It wouldn't hurt you to wear some of the things that other girls wear."

"If you're an A cup and you wear a bra, you're only doing it for emotional support."

My mother laughs. "I only want you to keep an open mind."

She laughs because she thinks I was trying to be funny, but I wasn't. "My mind is too open. Everything is in it. Nothing is left out."

"I don't understand."

"Nothing comes first." Of course I mean all the colors and all the mirrors and all the *sale* signs and mannequins mixed in everywhere with the real people. There are stereos running and a washing machine or two and twelve television sets in a row showing the Smurfs in different sizes. There is a data level I can't comprehend or turn down. But how do you communicate about a whizzed-up brain?

She shows me a rack of sweaters ranging from $34 to $44. Then a rack of paisley print sweatshirts starting at $30.

"You could get some dark slacks to go with them."

"They cost too much and they're not me. I wish I could tell you what it's like but I can't. I can't get anything sorted out." My dad would hate these clothes and what they stand for. Fashion is just a way of circulating money. It's a game you shouldn't play because it's a game you can't win; it's a walk on the treadmill of the Amerikan way. There is so much noise. I can't get scrambled, though. I *will* myself not to get scrambled.

"Mother, please, let's go to a smaller store or the voice will come."

"All right. Just be calm."

"There must be a quiet one, without any stereo."

"I'm sure there is. Let's go find it."

34

We walk straight ahead. My pulse is racing and all the stores make a data glut, but if I keep my eyes front and walk straight I'll be okay. We go into a store called *Glamour Isle*. There are mirrors everywhere, even on the ceiling. It makes me tense; it seems to multiply the data. The store specializes in expensive fashions for young women. But I don't complain; I know my mother wants to do what's best for me. At least it's quiet.

Mother is looking through a rack of sale sweaters. From the corner of my eye, I see a salesgirl approaching; suddenly, my stomach forms a sharp knot. It is DeeDee, my lab partner from biology.

She has a wide smile. "Hi. It's a small world, huh?"

Now what am I going to do? I feel myself flushing madly but there's no way out. I'm too embarrassed to look her in the eye. "Hi," I mumble.

"You know each other?" my mother wants to know.

"We're in biology together," says DeeDee. "We're lab partners."

"How nice," my mother says. She looks at me like I'm supposed to say something. She doesn't know that this girl has seen me get scrambled.

DeeDee starts showing us merchandise. At least it's an attention shift. She shows us stirrup pants for $18, and fleece-lined stirrup pants for $24, and stirrup pants with matching suspenders for $30.

"Stirrup pants are in," she says. "They're real nice with striped sweaters, whether you wear the suspenders or not."

She knows what's in; it would be so natural for her. I don't have much interest in the clothes, but a lot in her. Where does a person get such composure? She doesn't have a moment of fear, even though she's never spoken with my mother before. Her skin has a healthy tan glow and her hair is thick and rich and blond. I would like to stand in a corner somewhere and watch her.

She shows us some knee-length sweater dresses. I would never wear one, but I like the colors, turquoise, peach, plum, powder

35

blue. "These are good with stirrup pants," says DeeDee. "If you had black stirrup pants, any of these colors would be nice."

I can't stand the attention. I turn away. My lump is dissolving, but I'm still tense. I would like to be left alone. Her life must be very sound, but do I look like the kind of person who wears a sweater skimp?

Mother and I sort through the racks of fifty- and sixty-dollar designer jeans. I have to choose something to get this over with. I finally find a pair of brushed denim Levis, and a yellow Looney Tunes tee shirt for $3.99 on a sale table.

DeeDee does the cash register and takes my mother's check. As soon as she looks at the check she says, "Hey, it's a small world again. We live in the same neighborhood."

"We do?" asks my mother.

"We live on Roosevelt, about a block and a half west of MacArthur. We're neighbors, practically."

She is looking at me but I don't look up. I don't want this; if only I could wear my old blue jeans and Uncle Larry's fatigue jacket and somehow turn invisible.

DeeDee is putting the clothes in a *Glamour Isle* shopping bag. "It's nice to meet you," she tells my mother. And then she says to me, "I'll see you Monday." But she is talking with static.

The clothes are in the bag, so I put the bag under my arm. "See you Monday," I murmur. I walk quickly out of the store, watching my toes; I am taking tiny, rapid steps. Mother chases after me and catches up on a wooden bench which forms an octagon around some potted trees.

"I don't want this to be an ordeal for you, Grace; I really don't."

"I know." I'm gulping air.

"Shopping for something new can be a real pick-me-up if you could only loosen up. Besides, you can't go for the rest of your life in tee shirts and blue jeans and your uncle's fatigue jacket."

"I know, Mother, but please don't talk about Uncle Larry. I know you're right, but the problem's not a matter of *understanding*. I need some deep breaths."

"Maybe it *is* a problem of understanding," she says. "The girl in the store was just being friendly. Don't shut her out."

"She was getting too close. It would never work. I could never have a friend named DeeDee."

"You won't have any friends at all if you don't try."

"I couldn't explain it to you. A girl named DeeDee could stand naked in the locker room without a moment of stress."

"What is that supposed to mean?"

"Please drop it, Mother. Can't you see I need to breathe? It just wouldn't work. She wouldn't like me if she got to know me. No one does. When you're crazy wild, you don't have friends."

"I want you to stop it. You're not crazy wild."

We have lunch at McDonald's. Mother has a cheeseburger, and I have the chef's salad. I have to pick out the little chunks of ham and the bacon bits. I don't know if the bacon bits are really a meat by-product or if they're something artificial, but I'm not taking any chances. I eat about half the salad.

When we get home, I sit out on the balcony, in my niche. It is a hot, hot Saturday afternoon. I am mostly hidden but I have a field of vision between the draped towels.

Mr. Stereo has his pup tied to a scrawny tree near his patio. The tree grows in a small seam of gravel between this parking lot and the next one. I know it is a Russian olive tree because I looked it up in a tree book my dad and I used to use in the woods and fields. Such a lovely name for such a pitiful, lonely, shapeless tree. How could it be otherwise? Its soil is gravel and litter. I can't imagine an olive growing on it and I'm sure it will never have a mourning dove in its branches.

Watching the Surly People is like digging at a festering wound; it frightens me and yet I can't stop myself. I could hide in my room, I suppose, but the sky blows around and speaks with a firm whisper: *It's important to know everything. The Surly People are no accident.*

How the sky finds its quiet voice in the midst of all this noise I do not know. Mr. Stereo's patio speaker is loud and there are two or three others blaring in the parking lot. Every once in a while someone sets off a firecracker or a whole string of them.

At least a dozen people have found spots for sunbathing in the parking lot. Some of them are sitting in lawn chairs and others are lying on the hoods or tops of cars. Everyone drinks beer and smokes cigarettes. Every once in a while, a new car arrives, spilling out stereo noise and loud people. The people stay long enough to drink a beer or two, and then they leave, their engines roaring and their tires squealing.

A girl named Brenda and her friend Irene are sunbathing on top of an old, corroded Dodge. The car radio is loud through the open windows. Five or six boys are draped over the car or leaning up against it. Somehow, they can enjoy their own noise and screen out the rest. Most of them go to West High; I have seen them there. One of them, whose name is DeWayne, is working on a motorcycle next to the car. His shirt is off and one side of his face is disfigured with burn-scar tissue. One of his eyebrows curves up instead of down; he frightens me. It isn't hard to know information about them. They spray their lives around like a hose.

The girl named Brenda sits up on top of the car. The top of her bikini is untied and for a moment her large breasts swing free. She covers herself nonchalantly and reties the top while DeWayne lights her cigarette. I wonder if anything ever intimidates her. There must be something in me which admires the Surly People and their fearless assault on life.

It could be that the trash is worse than the noise. The noise comes and goes but the trash is constant. The beer bottles are

38

everywhere, and the beer cans, the pop cans, Styrofoam Big Mac boxes, broken glass, cigarette packs, candy wrappers. It would take most of a notebook to make a complete list. There are discarded rolls of carpet which slope away from the dumpster like foothills.

It would be rewarding to take a garbage bag and pick up litter, but I am afraid.

After supper, I do some homework at the kitchen table. I can see through the open back door that Mr. Stereo's pup has wrapped his chain around the tree many times so he has no slack.

If I fixed the chain, the dog would have some freedom of movement. The only people in the parking lot are on the far side, and Mr. Stereo is not on his patio. But he would be able to watch me through his kitchen window. My pulse starts to race just thinking about it. But even in the Surly World there must be some small space for compassion.

Shall I part my hair behind?
Do I dare to eat a peach?

There can't be any harm in fixing the chain, I decide. I ease myself out the door and walk to the tree. The pup jumps up and down with enthusiasm and tries to wag his tail stump. Without looking to the right or left, I fix the chain.

When I start back to the door, I find that the pup can now reach the very edge of our patio. I squat down and he puts his front paws up on my knee. The cardboard disc he wears whacks my chin. I scratch him along the chin while he licks my face. For a moment, I have a peaceful, lovely feeling.

Suddenly, Mr. Stereo is standing over us. I sense his presence before he speaks; maybe I have seen his shadow out of the corner of my eye.

"Don't be doin' that."

His voice is charged with static and my heart starts to pound. I

39

don't dare look up; the fear freezes me. The panic takes me, because if I get scrambled, I won't be able to move at all.

"I said, don't be doin' that. I'm trainin' him to be a watchdog."

His voice is like the shorted radio; the words pop in and out. I'm paralyzed with panic. As soon as I let go of the dog I try to say, "I didn't mean any harm," but my mouth is dry as cotton and the words catch in my throat. I am starting to shake. I am absurd squatting here, and if I freeze here any longer it will only get worse. I can't look in his face.

Somehow, I get to my feet and make it inside. I close the back door and lean back against it, trying to get my breath. My heart is pounding like a hammer; surely it will split my chest open. My life can't be like this, all I did was fix the chain. What he means by watchdog training is probably something cruel.

I am so faint I get on the floor on my hands and knees. Mother is doing laundry in the basement. I pray to die of a heart attack, here and now. Please don't come upstairs, Mother. I don't want you to find me like this, and I could never explain about the dog's chain. If only I could be an insect. The mist is coming and I can't stop it.

Three

MY FIRST TIME in evening group is disorienting. I've never been in the hospital annex before, and I don't know any of the people. All the group members are teenagers; I think some of them may go to my high school, but I don't see any faces I recognize.

We sit on folding chairs in a small circle in a large room. I can see the hospital across the courtyard; the light is on in Dr. Rowe's office. It might be so reassuring to be back in the hospital but I know I'm not supposed to think that way.

Most of the people in the group speak of drugs and alcohol, which I know nothing about. The group leader, Mr. Carlson, seems old and tired. A girl named Wanda is monopolizing the conversation. She is fat and overbearing, smoking one cigarette after another; she talks about her stepfather's abuse and her own drinking problem. At least her problems are real.

It would be a relief if they just ignored me, but I know they won't. Sooner or later, I'll have to talk. It would be too embarrassing to talk about my hospital history, and where would I begin? I got scrambled twice the first day of school. It would be so desperate to try and talk about Mr. Stereo's pup.

Just when it seems as if Wanda will monopolize the conversation right to the end, Mr. Carlson cuts her off and turns to me.

"Grace, is there something you'd like to share with the group?"

I can feel myself starting to shake. I keep my face down.

"Since this is your first night, maybe you'd like to tell us a little bit about yourself."

He has static. If I clamp my hands between my knees, it may help. My brain is racing wildly, I have to say something. I swallow and say, "I hope we don't have to dissect frogs."

God, what an insane remark! Nobody says anything and I can feel my face burning.

Mr. Carlson asks me what I mean.

"In biology. My lab partner says there's no dissection until second semester. But what if there is? I don't think I could stand it."

Wanda speaks up immediately. She says students have rights. "I read about this girl in California," she says loudly. "Her and her mother sued the high school because it was against their religion to dissect animals. They won their case, too."

Stand up for your rights. It seems like such a thought, but Wanda would probably be capable of it.

Mr. Carlson smiles at me. "If you don't feel like going to court, maybe you could just speak to your counselor at school. There should be a way for you to transfer to another science class."

I nod my head but don't speak. He seems kind.

"In any case, it sounds like you've got plenty of time to sort it out, maybe an entire semester."

I nod again. My breathing is mostly restored. Mr. Carlson's life is so sound, is there a secret elixir? Since our time is up, I won't have to talk anymore.

In the TV lounge, I find my mother. She is working on lesson plans.

"How did it go?" she wants to know.

"Mr. Carlson is nice," I say. "I didn't get scrambled."

"You'll feel more comfortable when you get to know the other people."

"It sounds logical, Mother."

42

"Give it some time."

"Can we go home now? I'm so tired."

*

When Mother and I make gazpacho, I mince the vegetables while she seasons the broth. She is adding garlic, oregano, and basil to two quarts of tomato juice, while I am mincing onions, cucumbers, celery, and green peppers. Gazpacho is good to pack in a lunch because you can eat it cold.

I am listless with the knife. In the hospital, sharp objects are off-limits, even ballpoints. I have been flat out for almost a week. It is Mother's idea to make the soup; she hopes it will help me snap out of it.

"Gazpacho was one of Dad's favorites," I say.

"I know, Grace."

"You loved him, didn't you, Mother?"

"Of course I loved him."

"I'd like to use the mason jar for my soup. You can use the Thermos."

"That's fine with me; I like the Thermos better anyway."

As soon as we put the gazpacho to simmer, I go up to my room. I look at my nails; some of them are long and some are short, but the long ones are dirty. I could clean them with the nail brush, but they still wouldn't be the same size. I could cut the long ones so that they would all be the same size, but where would I find the nail clippers? They're never where they're supposed to be, and I don't have the energy to hunt for them. When I'm flat out, my entire body is drained of every spark of energy. Nothing matters, nothing makes any difference, nothing is worth the effort.

I don't know which is worse, being flat out or getting scrambled. When I get scrambled, it is terrifying and disorienting; when I'm

43

flat out, everything seems dull and hopeless. I was flat out when I tried to kill myself. The truth is, what's worse is what's current, but what's current never lasts.

The most pleasant thing is the aftermath of being scrambled, after the mist dissipates, when everything I see is spent and like a dream.

I hear the doorbell ring. It's only the second time I've heard it since we've lived here. I can hear my mother talking with someone at the front door, and then she calls up to me.

"Grace, you've got company."

I don't understand; I can feel my pulse quicken.

"Grace, please come downstairs. Someone is here to see you."

I go down slowly. It's DeeDee, my lab partner. In the store at the mall, she tried to get close.

"I wrote down your address from your check," she says to my mother. Then she turns to me. "I thought I'd say hello. I hope you don't mind."

I'm speechless, so my mother says, "It's very thoughtful of you."

The knot is forming in my stomach. This will only make things worse, I tried to warn my mother. This will only prolong the agony. DeeDee will spend just enough time with me to find out how truly weird I am, and then she will realize I'm a good person to avoid. There must be some way to save us both the trouble. Maybe the three of us will just stand here by the door for a minute or two and be polite, and then DeeDee will go home.

But my mother says, "Grace, why don't you show DeeDee your room?"

My room is just a room. I can't imagine why anyone would want to see it, but we go up anyway. DeeDee sits on the edge of my bed, and I sit on the chair by the desk.

"We only live about three blocks from here," she tells me. "Our house is on Roosevelt, about a block on the other side of MacArthur."

44

"The other side of MacArthur is a different world," I say.

She says something, but I don't hear what it is. Her beauty intimidates me. She is wearing olive green shorts with matching top. Her legs are golden brown like the rest of her clear skin; her blond hair is lovely. My own hair, when it's clean, has a deep red tone in the light, but mostly it's just mousy and clumpy.

DeeDee wants to know about my metal sculpture.

"My dad made it. He welded it."

"What does your dad do?"

"He's dead."

"Oh, I'm sorry."

"He died of fulminating leukemia. He was very well and then all of a sudden he was very sick. The whole thing only took six days. Now you see him, now you don't." There has to be a better way of talking to someone; why am I saying these things?

"I'm real sorry," she says. "Sometimes I put my foot in my mouth."

"It's okay." I am very uncomfortable. It's not fair to expect me to make conversation; I hope we're not going to have long, embarrassing silences.

I tell her that my mom is teaching at Stevenson School. It seems appropriate for polite conversation.

"I didn't go to Stevenson myself," says DeeDee, "but I have a lot of friends who did."

If you have someone in your home, you should get them something. I could offer her some gazpacho, but that's absurd; it isn't even cooked yet. I start to panic but then I remember about the Pepsi. "We have Pepsi in our refrigerator," I say quickly. "I'll get you one."

"You don't have to."

"Oh yes, please, it's perfect. I couldn't offer you any gazpacho, it's not ready yet." I go quickly. I get her a Pepsi and pour it into

45

a glass of ice and bring it up. I think DeeDee's poise is astonishing. She walks directly through the midst of the Surly People and knocks on the door of a stranger. "You must have complete self-assurance," I tell her.

"Not really," she says. She sits up straighter and for the first time, she seems a little uncomfortable. There is some red in her face. She takes a small drink from her glass and says, "Can I be honest with you?"

I feel my knot forming again. What does she mean?

"Miss Shapiro asked me if I'd come visit you."

Miss Shapiro? Miss Shapiro is the counselor at school.

DeeDee is holding her glass in both hands. She goes on, "I don't want to hurt your feelings, I'd like to get to know you and all that, but this was her idea."

"Miss Shapiro wears too much lipstick and I think she doesn't have much experience. She probably means well. Are you close to her?"

"I'm in water ballet, and she's the sponsor. She thought you could use a friend, since you're new in school and everything. She asked me if I'd visit you and sort of show you the ropes at school. She was going to tell you later on, but it doesn't seem honest if I don't say anything. I'm sorry."

I can feel myself flushing. This is so embarrassing, but it stands to reason. Why else would a girl like DeeDee try to make contact with someone like me?

"I'll leave if you want; I wouldn't blame you."

"No, please." It's so confusing, now I'm a project. This could be even worse. She said since I'm new *and everything;* Miss Shapiro knows my medical history, has she shared it with DeeDee?

"I'm sorry about the Pepsi," I blurt out. "I should've gotten one for both of us, so you wouldn't have to drink yours alone. It puts you

46

in an awkward situation. I don't like Pepsi, though, so it would be phony."

"Don't worry about it, I'm fine."

She drinks some more Pepsi and sets the glass down. She smiles and says, "It must be hard moving away from all your friends and everything."

And everything? Why does she say it again? "I've never had many friends. It's hard for me to make friends. After my dad died, Mother took courses to get a current certificate. This is the first teaching job she's ever had. Please, can you tell me what Miss Shapiro said about me?"

"She just said you're new in school and you've been in the hospital. She said you're shy. That's the whole story. I know it seems kind of artificial, but maybe we can still be friends. If you want."

I feel so confused all I can think to do is talk. "I have to repeat the tenth grade," I blurt out. "I missed too much school last year because I was in the hospital."

"Were you sick?" DeeDee asks.

"Yes, you might say sick. It was a mental hospital."

She looks down at her glass. "I'm sorry."

It's so much harder this way. Why did she have to come in the first place? "I was being treated for depression. Last fall, I tried to kill myself. It would have worked, but my mother found me too soon. The doctors said it was a delayed reaction to my father's death. I'm not sure if doctors really know a lot about mental illness, but they usually act like they do. My father and I were very close, maybe too close. It wasn't the first time I had depression, but it was the worst; it was the first time I ever tried to kill myself."

"Are you better now?"

"I'm sicker now. I've got schizophrenia now, besides the depression."

DeeDee's eyes are still down. I've made her uncomfortable. Maybe that's what I want, maybe that's why I'm carrying on like this. "I've heard of it," she says. "We don't have to talk about it if you don't want to."

"It's very terrifying. I wouldn't know how to explain it. Sometimes my doctor thinks I've got schizoaffective disorder. That's when you're depressed and schizo at the same time. It's quite confusing, especially from in here." It's so perverse the way I'm blabbing these things she doesn't need to know. There are tears stinging my eyes. Maybe I just want to make certain she doesn't come back.

It seems it will help if we change the subject. "Please, let's talk about science." It's not a smooth transition, but what do I know about social skills?

She tells me science is her favorite subject. After high school, she plans to go to the University of Illinois and then become a science teacher. I can see that she is in control; she will become what she wants to become.

I tell her that science has never been my best subject, but I like Miss Braverman. She likes Miss Braverman too.

"Do you have any special interest or do you just like science in general?" I ask.

"I like botany the best," says DeeDee. "I grow some shrubs and trees at home."

"I'm sure you must be very good at it." I'm not sure what I mean by that remark, but at least I'm not getting scrambled.

"Sometimes I think I'd like to have my own nursery," DeeDee says. "I like to dig in the dirt. It would be fun to grow ornamental trees and shrubs, then sell them for outrageous prices." She laughs.

48

I try to laugh too, but I'm too nervous. My deep breathing causes me to miss some of the conversation; all I know is, she's talking about the science fair and suitable projects.

When she has to leave, she says, "Would you like to walk to school together sometime?"

"I don't know if I could do that."

"Why not? You have to pass my house on your way."

"Please, I just wouldn't know. I'll give it some serious thought, I really will."

I watch her down the street through our kitchen window. My mother is cutting blue construction paper letters for her bulletin board at school.

I watch DeeDee all the way to MacArthur Street. Mr. Stereo has his loud friend and his loud stereo on his patio. His noise is annoying and confusing; I'm trying to think about DeeDee.

"It was nice of her to visit you," says my mother.

"When she graduates from college, she's going to be a science teacher."

"And what about you, Grace? What are you going to do?"

"I can't think about that. I don't dare. I have to think about surviving."

"Nonsense. You're not going to be sick forever. If you had a good friend, I doubt if things would seem so bad. Maybe you and DeeDee will become friends."

"I doubt that, Mother. She knows I'm wacko; I told her. She has such poise and her life is so sound."

"No one is perfect, Grace. I'm sure she has problems, like anyone else."

"The truth is, it wasn't even her idea to come here. It was Miss Shapiro's."

"What do you mean?"

49

I tell her the story and she says she's sorry. "I'm sure that's disappointing," she says.

"It's more than disappointing," I tell her. "Now she'll try to spend time with me, but it will be artificial. It will be just another source of discomfort."

"It doesn't have to be; the two of you might still be friends."

She doesn't understand. How could she? "DeeDee doesn't need friends," I tell her. "I'm a mission. I'm a project."

"Don't overreact. So she didn't come to visit you spontaneously. That doesn't mean the two of you can't enjoy each other."

I can't understand any of this. My mother is so supportive but the stereo is too loud. I'm going flat out again and I'm tired of talking. Why did DeeDee have to come?

"Does he have to play that stereo so loud? Can't we do something?"

"It's not as bad as it usually is," she says. "I could call the landlord, maybe."

"Please let's don't talk about it, Mother. Can I help you cut out letters?"

"Sure, if you want. The other scissors are on the telephone stand."

*

9/12

Dear Diary:

From my balcony I can see the beer bottles on the ground and in the street. Some of them are broken. There was a party last night in the neighborhood, except I couldn't really call it a party and I couldn't really call this a neighborhood. It was more like roving gangs. I watched it all from my niche. There were crowds of college students in the parking lot across the street, playing loud stereos and pouring beer. The Surly People threw beer bottles and firecrackers at them. At two in the morning, my mom called the police. The police came and directed a long line of traffic out onto MacArthur. It reminded me of parking lot traffic at the county fair.

I put the diary away and go into the bathroom. The next time I see Dr. Rowe, she will ask me about what I've written. I don't know if she wants to know about the Surly People; I could tell her things, but I'm not sure she would want to hear them. The cracked mirror splices my face; I can see my left eye twice and the tip of my nose twice. I need to hurry now; Mother is gone to school and I'm running late.

I lock the apartment and walk fast. I can't get to MacArthur Street without passing the IGA parking lot. Lots of Surly People are congregated there, near the curb. They are leaning on their cars, smoking cigarettes, drinking Pepsis, and eating candy bars. They hurl their trash around. They are lighting firecrackers and throwing them at each other.

They are the usual ones from our parking lot, and also many others. The one called DeWayne is there, and Brenda, and one called Butch, who has his hair cut very short with arrows shaved in it, right down to the scalp. Is he just bizarre, or is he evil?

I'm very afraid to walk in this place. There must be another route I could take to school, but 14th Street is a dead end. I walk faster; I try to go past the lot without looking to the right or to the left. I hope and pray that they will ignore me, but sometimes they don't.

"Woof woof. Hey, woof woof."

"Bow wow. Bow wow wow."

I can't look at them. I *mustn't* look. There is a burst of laughter, but I walk straight ahead. My heart is pounding wild in my chest and my legs are starting to shake. I shouldn't have written in the diary; writing in the diary made me late.

51

"Hey bow wow, here boy."

"Woof woof."

They are whistling as if to call a dog. There are more bursts of laughter. I make it to the corner but I have to wait for traffic; there are tears stinging my eyes and I'm starting to shake. I can still hear the loud whistles and the loud laughter. Why do they do this to me? What kind of cruelty is it?

I make it across the street, choking back my tears. All the way to school, I've still got the shakes; my brain is a chain of flashbulbs. Inside the school, I don't stop at my homeroom, I go straight to the bathroom. I have to pee so bad I'm afraid I'm going to wet my pants.

I get relief and wash my face in front of the mirror and the mist is coming: I'm going to get scrambled. Somehow, I make it to the library and sit among the stacks. Libraries are such safe places; I am scrambled in the mist but I am safe here. Anyway the aftermath will come and the world will have the aura of a dream.

When lunchtime comes, DeeDee sits with me. It is the first time I have eaten in the cafeteria instead of the homeroom. Does she sit with me because it's an assignment, or does she do it of her own free will? It seems demeaning but also comforting not to be alone. Maybe I've had so much institutional support I expect to be sponsored everywhere I go.

My head hurts but I tell DeeDee about the Surly People and the IGA parking lot.

"That's just Brenda Chitwood and the hoods that hang around her. Don't pay any attention to them, they're not worth it."

She has minor static. It's easy for her to say, her life is so sound she probably has no cavities when she goes to the dentist.

Two other girls join us, named Maureen and Diane. They start talking about cheerleader tryouts, and it will make me very happy if

52

they simply ignore me altogether. For a while they do, but then Maureen wants to know why I'm spooning gazpacho from a mason jar instead of eating school lunch.

"I'm vegetarian," I say quietly. I don't look up. I really hope the conversation will go back to cheerleading or some other subject.

"You mean you never eat any meat?"

"No."

"Why not?"

There is a little static in her voice but I answer the best I can, "I believe in animal rights. I don't think we have the right to butcher animals just because we have the power."

Diane says, "But you have to have protein. Meat is one of the basic food groups."

"There are better sources of protein, sources that don't include animal fats." I sound like such a prude. A prune, I mean. I don't mean to, but I'm so afraid when I talk to strangers. How can you hope to make friends if you behave like a prune? My dad was so good at this sort of thing — he could speak his mind and be warm and natural at the same time.

Maureen says, "You mean you never eat a Big Mac or anything?"

I don't have an answer. Mercifully, a cafeteria monitor asks us to move to make room for other people.

*

It is the next day, I think. I'm getting pretty sound on my days, maybe the medicine is helping me establish basic orientation. I lock the apartment and walk to the curb but there are beer bottles on the ground. I face the end of the street, clear to MacArthur. There is the IGA lot and I freeze; my heart starts to pound and my eyes are popping like flashbulbs. I need to get more sleep at night.

I look again to MacArthur Street. The clouds have swirled a

deadly canopy over 14th Street. A tunnel. I can't walk that way. I just can't, I just can't.

I walk up the parking lot past the dumpster, where I find a break in the chain link fence I can squeeze through. On the other side of the fence is a huge field of overgrown weeds and trash. With deep, deep breathing I start walking across the field, in the direction of the tract houses on the far side.

The clouds are flung around and I hear the noisy sky chatter. Sometimes words come and sometimes sentences. I have found an alternate route; it will take me at least three blocks out of my way, but there will be no Surly People.

This doesn't change a thing. The Surly People will not go away.

But I will go away from them; I won't have to endure their cruelty.

It is a mistake to think so. There are legions of them. The forces of darkness are everywhere.

The sky persists; it follows me on my walk across the field. The sun is the eye in the sky; it sees into every corner. I feel like a character in a Greek tragedy, and the sky is the chorus. But my life is too pitiful to be tragic. DeeDee will wait for me in front of her house, but I won't come.

"What do you want from me?" I ask the sky.

The forces of darkness are everywhere. Someone has to stand with the forces of light.

It is my father's voice the sky is using. I'm positive that he died. But other people don't hear it. It only shows how crazy wild I truly am. I would hate for people to see me talking to the sky.

"I could do a project for the science fair. I could make a display on animal rights."

It's a small gesture, but it's a beginning.

"I could do it on cruelty and animal rights. I have so much material."

54

Start small and then expand your range until you stand with the forces of light.

"DeeDee thinks I should do a science project. She may even want me for a friend, although I don't know why. She may feel that I have redeeming qualities."

There is no answer. The sky is gone. I'm glad I found this route; I will walk this way from now on. The sky may come again, but there are no Surly People.

After school, I walk home with DeeDee. She says she missed me this morning and I apologize. She wants to know if I've given any thought to a project for the science fair.

"I have thought about it," I admit. Of course I would never mention my conversation with the sky.

"Well, think about it some more," she says with a laugh.

"Okay, I will. I'll think about it some more."

When we get to her house, she unlocks the door and says, "Can you stay for a little while? As soon as I change, I'll get us some Seven-Up."

She wants me to stay; she wants to spend time with me. We walk through the kitchen and out into the double garage. She is showing me a two-door maroon Camaro with a sparkly, metallic finish.

"This is my car," she says. "At least it's *going* to be, as soon as my dad finishes some brake work on it."

"It's very nice, DeeDee. It looks like a sports car."

"It used to belong to my brother, but he bought this four-door, cream-colored Volvo. My dad bought the Camaro from him and gave it to me for my birthday."

I don't know how to talk about cars. "Where's your brother?" I ask.

"He's a senior in college. He thinks a Volvo is more *him*."

It makes me so nervous to try and hold up my end of a conversation. The garage is still and hot. I look around at all the tools which are hung with so much care and the ten-speed bicycles suspended from the ceiling. I love the familiar, musty smell of stale grease and oil; the garden shop at Allerton smelled this way. I would like to tell DeeDee how comforting the smell is, but that's the kind of remark which makes people nervous.

"Do you have a driver's license, DeeDee?"

"Sure, don't you?"

Her eyes are so clear and blue. I look away quickly. "I never took behind-the-wheel. I missed out on it when I was in the hospital."

"So? Just take it this year then."

"I'm not sure I could, it would frighten me to drive a car. There's so much data I'm afraid I would get scrambled."

"You can get a license, just like anybody else. There's nothing to it, really. C'mon, let's go upstairs."

"I think your car is real nice, DeeDee."

I sit on the edge of DeeDee's bed while she changes. Her room is very large and very nice. There is thick carpeting and she has a poster of Mikhail Baryshnikov on her wall. "You have a nice house," I say.

She shrugs her shoulders. "It's okay, I guess." She has taken off her blouse and skirt and her half-slip. She is hanging up her skirt and blouse on hangers with clips, wearing only her white underpants and her crisp white bra. I feel myself starting to flush; I wonder if I should look away.

It's going to feel less tense if I talk. "Before we moved here, we had a lovely stone house," I tell her. "It was built in 1840. The walls were about a foot thick and the house had exposed walnut beams and door latches instead of door knobs. My dad modernized it, but he knew how to blend the new with the old. My Uncle Larry helped him with some of the remodeling. Uncle Larry was killed in

56

action in Vietnam. His name is on the Vietnam memorial in Washington, D.C." Why am I jabbering like this?

DeeDee is feeding the fish in a large aquarium near her window; she is still wearing only her underwear. The aquarium has a filter and fluorescent lights. She feeds the fish from a vial that looks like a salt shaker. "I'm sorry about your uncle," she says. "The house sounds real special. It sounds like it had lots of character."

I feel confident that she won't take her underwear off; she won't do that. No one could be that unself-conscious. "Our house was at Allerton Park," I tell her.

"Your house was in a park?"

"Not exactly in a park. Our house was on the Allerton estate. Allerton Park is about fifteen hundred acres, but the estate is almost five thousand acres. Most of the estate is farms; our house was right beside a dairy farm."

"Fifteen hundred acres is really big. What kind of a park was it?"

"It's not a park like a city park. There's a huge Georgian mansion and European formal gardens. There are hiking paths through the woods. There are so many statues, I wish I could show them to you. Some of the statues are bronze and concrete, but some are alabaster."

DeeDee is putting on a pair of designer jeans and a pale blue sweater. She looks at herself briefly in the full-length, crystal-clear mirror mounted on her closet door. I like telling her about our stone house. I like it that I can share with her. I would like to believe that we will become friends, but it may be dangerous to think that way.

"Our house is expensive," she says, "but it doesn't have any character. It's just the same as all the other houses in the neighborhood. Sometimes I even think the way we live doesn't have any character."

"Please, I don't think I understand."

"My parents are into materialism." She sits on the corner of the bed and starts running the brush through her thick hair. "When I hear you talk about your father, I feel jealous. You were close to him, and he stood for something. People like that make the world a better place."

I can't imagine myself as the object of anyone's envy, especially hers. I shrug my shoulders and don't say anything.

DeeDee goes on, "My parents are concerned about keeping their social calendar straight at the country club and having the Liqui-Green man come over once a week to treat the lawn with all the right chemicals."

"I don't want to argue, DeeDee, but isn't that the way most people want to live?"

She sighs. "I guess so. My brother is going to be just like my parents. He can't wait to be a yuppie."

"Don't be too hard on your family, though, please. People do things. They do things to survive."

She looks at me with a puzzled expression.

"Please don't think I'm criticizing you. It's just something I've learned from being in the looney bin. A lot of people are hanging on for dear life; hanging by their fingernails. People do what they have to do to survive."

She is frowning but she says, "I'll have to think about it."

Who am I to tell her a better way of thinking? Who am I to be the giver of advice? I can feel my pulse beginning to race; it was probably a mistake to bring up the mental illness.

"Come on," she says to me. "Let's go downstairs."

I leave to go home at five o'clock, when DeeDee is getting ready to go to work at the mall. I walk very fast along the sidewalk and keep a close watch on my feet. It will be safe to walk

58

past the IGA now, it's past five o'clock and the Surly People will be gone.

*

It is three days later when DeeDee is waiting by my locker after school. I put some books away.

"Let's go talk to Miss Braverman," she says. She still thinks I should do a project. I'd like to, but I don't think I could get one finished.

"I don't think I could," I say.

"Sure you can."

I feel a touch of dizziness. "DeeDee, I don't mean to offend you, but why are you doing this? I'm sorry, but I have to ask."

"What do you mean?"

"You're giving me all this encouragement in science. Please tell me it's not Miss Shapiro's idea."

"No way."

"Because if it's just part of Miss Shapiro's strategy, it would be so humiliating."

"This doesn't have anything to do with Miss Shapiro; I only talked to her that one time."

"I don't want to seem ungrateful. I'm only bringing it up because in a way it would be better to be ignored than to be someone's project."

Her eyes are so kind when she looks at me. "I'm really sorry. I should've just kept my mouth shut about Miss Shapiro."

"Oh no, you were just being honest."

She smiles and says, "This is just my idea. If you get involved in the science fair, I think you'll really like it. Please believe me."

I do believe her. "I do believe you," I say. She does act like she wants me for a friend, the way she's so kind and encouraging.

59

I take a deep breath. "Okay then, let's go."

We go to Miss Braverman's room. I am standing next to her desk while DeeDee sits in one of the front row desks.

"What's on your mind, Grace?" Miss Braverman's smile is kind, but she is so chic and she has such composure. She will see through me; she will know how unstable I am and how incompetent.

I swallow and say, "I would like to do a project for the science fair."

"What kind of project would you like to do?"

"I would like to do it on cruelty to animals in laboratory experiments. It would be an information display." There, I said it.

Miss Braverman crosses her arms and tugs at her earlobe. "You catch me by surprise," she says.

A small knot forms in my stomach.

She goes on, "I don't want to discourage you, Grace, but it sounds as though it might be a little on the negative side. A display on cruelty to animals in laboratories might put scientific investigation in a bad light."

"I understand." Some of her words are beginning to pop with static.

"Usually, projects for the science fair have something to do with research and development or scientific progress. Do you see what I mean? It's usually a positive approach."

"I understand." Her voice is popping out. Why is DeeDee sitting at that desk instead of standing here beside me? She's the one who urged this on me.

Miss Braverman says, "If you did this particular project, you would need to put the emphasis on the scientific aspect and not on the political or emotional aspect. It would be good, for example, to show the goals of certain experiments and how those same goals might be achieved without using laboratory animals."

"Miss Braverman, please, I need to sit down."

60

I sit in the chair next to her desk and take deep breaths. DeeDee and Miss Braverman hover over me like clucking hens. DeeDee wants to know if I need a glass of water. I am so pathetic I almost laugh at myself. Miss Braverman says there's a lot of flu going around, she has no idea how whacked out I am.

*

We are outside, walking home. I've still got the shakes, somewhat.

"Are you going to be okay?" DeeDee asks.

"I will be, sooner or later."

"Have you always been like this, Grace?"

"More or less. Not exactly. Not this bad."

"Miss Braverman didn't turn you down."

"I know."

When we get to DeeDee's house, we go into the family room. There are two more aquariums like the one in her room; she is feeding the fish again. The family room has expensive, rust-colored carpeting. There are large paintings of cats, in Japanese style, with chrome frames.

All done feeding the fish, DeeDee sits beside me on the couch. She wants to know about my mental illness. "If you think I should mind my own business, just tell me," she says.

A small, hard lump forms, causing me to hesitate. I do want her for a friend but how close can I let her get?

"I tried to kill myself September twelfth of last year. It was three months exactly after my dad died. I got home from school at about four o'clock on the bus, like any other day. Mother was gone, she was running some errands. I changed my clothes and sat out on our flagstone patio; it was a beautiful sunny day with the bluest sky and a touch of fall in the air. I happened to look at our pile of firewood, which was close to my chair. The pile of logs was so small, and it was clear to me that it wouldn't last long. I'd been depressed all

61

day, but for some reason that pile of firewood made me feel all hollow inside like there wasn't anything worth living for. I knew my dad would never be coming home again and the two of us would never go out in the woods again to gather firewood. It felt like this huge prison of sadness, and I knew that death would set me free."

"How did you do it?" DeeDee asks. Her elbows are on her knees and her chin is in her hands. She's a good listener.

"I cut my wrists with a razor blade, in the bathtub. Actually, I only cut my left wrist. There were single-edge razor blades in my dad's art supplies in his old desk. I was unconscious when my mom got home and found me, but I was still alive."

"Then what happened?"

"I went into the hospital. I was in for a little more than six weeks, clear up to the end of October. I got ECT treatments and everything."

"What's ECT?"

"Shock treatments. They wire you up and zap you. They're horrible. My new doctor, Dr. Rowe, doesn't give shock treatments to teenagers."

"I'm sorry, Grace, I really am."

"Then in January I went back in for another month. I had another ECT series."

"What about the schizophrenia?"

"The schizophrenia started this summer when we started getting ready to move. The most horrible, confusing things started happening to me. I started having these terrible nightmares and I would wake up screaming and sweating; sometimes I even wet the bed. Every once in a while I would hear these voices speaking to me, and sometimes the voices were like my father's voice; sometimes the voices would come from out of the sky. My mom and my grandma couldn't hear the voices, only I could hear them. I had a lot of trouble sleeping every night, and I didn't have any appetite.

62

When I wasn't disoriented, I was just depressed. It got worse after we moved here. We were only here about a month when I found myself in another looney bin."

"It sounds like the schizophrenia came so sudden."

"That's true, but Dr. Rowe says your chances of getting better are increased if it happens that way. There's almost no chance of getting well if you have the slow kind, the progressive kind. I don't understand what all of it means, but that's what she tells me."

"I can see how scary it is for you, Grace, I'm sorry if I was prying."

"It isn't prying, you're just open. It's the most wonderful quality." She makes it possible for me to share. I would like to give her a hug, but I wouldn't know how to do a thing like that.

DeeDee gets us each a Seven-Up and we go out to sit on her patio. She shows me a lilac bush she has been pruning and a variegated red twig dogwood she has recently planted. I tell her briefly about the scraggly Russian olive tree near our apartment. She says a tree that far gone would probably need lots of pruning and some work with a deep-root feeder.

She has an Irish setter named Rowdy; we throw a rubber ball around the yard and he romps after it. I lie in the grass and hold my arms around him. His fur is soft and warm and he slurps my chin with his scratchy tongue.

"He's the nicest dog, DeeDee."

"You like dogs."

"I love dogs. Mother says our apartment is no place to have a dog, but I'd give anything if we could. When we lived in the country we had a big malamute we named Tubba, which was short for tub of lard. He was overweight. We had to leave him with my grandma, but at least I know he has a nice home." I have tears forming when I think of Tubba, but I blink them back.

"Rowdy is a stitch sometimes. Watch this." She drops the ball straight down and he crawls on his belly, all the way across the patio.

I start to laugh. He does it again and I am laughing even harder, and it feels so good to laugh.

DeeDee puts away the ball and asks me if I want more Seven-Up.

The sky is blue and the sun is so warm. "No thanks, I have plenty." We are sitting on comfortable redwood patio furniture.

"There's plenty more if you change your mind."

"No, I'm fine." It's mellow sitting here with her. "DeeDee, sometimes I think of having tea with Miss Braverman."

"What do you mean?"

"In my imagination. It's a fantasy. I picture you and me going together to have tea with her in her apartment, on a Sunday afternoon. Is it okay if I tell you this?"

She is scratching Rowdy around the ears. "Sure, why not?"

"It's just such a weird thought. I have so many weird thoughts, but I feel like I can share it with you."

"It doesn't seem so weird, tell me about it."

I take a moment to moisten my lips. "Miss Braverman's apartment is real tasteful. She serves us tea on a slate coffee table, with real china cups and saucers. The cream pitcher and sugar bowl are also china, with gold leaf trim."

DeeDee is smiling, but she doesn't say anything.

I go ahead, "It is the late part of the afternoon, when things are mellow, when people usually get a little drowsy. She's not a teacher, and we aren't high school students. We are just three women, having tea together."

"What do we talk about?" she wants to know.

"We only talk about sophisticated, high-minded subjects like art and literature and the theater. The three of us are very sophisticated."

64

"It's a nice picture," she says. "I don't see why you were afraid to tell me about it."

"I wasn't really afraid, not completely. It's just that I have such thoughts sometimes; I like the smell in your garage and I love to hear the mourning dove. I know I'm different, but I don't want people to think I'm weird. If you're real weird, you can't make friends."

"There's nothing weird about it; it would be fun to talk to Miss Braverman as an equal."

"You really mean that? When I think of having tea together it seems comforting and reassuring."

"I don't think it's weird," she says again. Suddenly she gets silly and raises her eyebrows two or three times. "You should hear some of *my* fantasies."

"I'd love to, what are they?"

Now she is laughing out loud. "I'll never tell."

"You can tell me, it's okay."

She is still laughing and shaking her head. "Oh no. I'll never tell, no way."

I start laughing too, although I'm not sure why. But it feels so good, who cares?

DeeDee finally says, "I have to go to work!"

When I get home, my mom is already there. "I've had the most wonderful day, Mother."

"Where have you been?"

"At DeeDee's house. Were you worried?"

"I wouldn't say worried, exactly. But you're always home before I am."

"I've had the most wonderful day. I talked to Miss Braverman about doing a project for the science fair; I almost got scrambled but I didn't. Then I went home with DeeDee. We had the nicest talk;

65

I told her things about myself I didn't think I could ever tell anyone."

"She seems like a lovely girl, Grace."

"I think she likes me; I really do. She thinks I have redeeming qualities."

"Why shouldn't she think it? You *do* have redeeming qualities; lots of them."

"I think we might turn out to be friends, Mother, I really do. I might even do a project for the science fair."

"I hope you will."

"Things are going to get better, Mother; I can tell."

*

I have finished my project for the science fair; I have worked on it every night this week, and it is done. I have included some of the most hideous experiments done on creatures, such as crushing live monkeys' skulls in an electric vise, and birthing puppies from starved mothers. I have tried to minimize the politics and maximize the so-called scientific aspect, the way Miss Braverman asked me to do.

The project is a display on four large pieces of white posterboard, twenty-four by thirty inches each. The posterboard panels stand upright in cardboard frames which I made. There are lots of photographs, and I did the lettering in calligraphy, using my dad's pen sets and guide books. My dad would be proud of this project.

After school, I take the project to Miss Braverman's room, but she is not there. The door is locked; a note says she will be back at 3:45. I can't wait till 3:45, because I have to make up my laps. I carry the display under my arm and walk to the P.E. wing.

I tell the P.E. secretary I'm supposed to make up my swimming laps now, but she says, "I don't know where Mrs. DeSmet is right now."

"But please, I'm supposed to make up my laps."

"Why didn't you do them in P.E.?"

"I got scrambled."

"What is that supposed to mean?" Her voice has lots of static.

"Please, I need to talk to her."

Then Mrs. DeSmet comes in. Mercifully. I catch my breath while she tells me to get changed into my suit and meet her at the pool.

I am the only one in the locker room. While I am changing quickly into my suit, I glance at myself in the large mirror above the lavatories. I seem smoky in the mirror because it isn't made of glass, it's the metal kind mounted at an angle so that people in wheelchairs can see themselves. I stack my display next to my locker.

Mrs. DeSmet is sitting on a folding chair next to the swimming pool, reading a book called *Her Only Sin* and eating from a bag of Fritos. The water in the pool is so utterly calm that I can see the exact contours of the lines painted on the bottom.

Mrs. DeSmet tells me not to worry about speed, just get the laps done. I start swimming and the water is warm and clear and still; it is ever so peaceful and reassuring. I swim the laps and I wish they could go on forever. Maybe Mrs. DeSmet will get bored and leave, and I will just swim on through a time warp and into another plane. Poetry goes through my head as I go:

> *The laps are lovely, clear and deep,*
> *But I have promises to keep.*

Mrs. DeSmet is telling me to get out of the pool. "You've done fifteen now; you only needed to do twelve."

I grip the edge of the pool. "It's so pleasant swimming the laps."

"I'm glad you like it, but the test is twelve laps."

I know what the promises are. "I have to take my science project to Miss Braverman," I say.

67

"That sounds good. Please get dressed, Grace."

After I am dressed, I climb the stairs from the locker room. Swimming the laps has refreshed me.

I go through the door into the hallway, and I freeze.

In front of me are half a dozen Surly People, and I recognize three of them: Brenda Chitwood, the one called DeWayne, and the one called Butch. They are spray painting black swastikas on the lockers.

Fear has gripped me like a vise, but their backs are toward me; I make a panicky grab at the door, hoping I can slip back through it without making any noise. But I am too late. The door swings shut with a loud clunk and the startled Surly People turn on me.

"Well, well, look who's here."

"I'll be damned if it's not Woof Woof."

"Hey bow wow."

My heart is pounding so wild in my chest that it drives out my breath. The hallway is tight and narrow; I grab at the doorknob behind me, but the one called Butch snatches my wrist with such force that it feels it will break.

"Oh God no, please no."

He is twisting my arm behind my back. "It's too bad you had to see this, Bow wow. You might get the not-so-bright idea to tell somebody about it, and I don't think MacFarlane would appreciate our art work."

The one called DeWayne laughs loudly. "Probably not," he says. He presses me against the wall and holds my chin in his hand. He is so powerful. The burned-out eyebrow is terrifying. "You wouldn't want to tell MacFarlane about our art work, would you, Woof Woof?"

"I'll bet she would," says Butch. "I'll bet she just loves show and tell."

I want to tell them no, I'll never tell a soul, but I don't have any breath to speak with. I can feel the tears rolling down my face.

"I'll bet we've got some show and tell right here," says Butch; he snatches my posterboard displays. DeWayne grips my chin and forces my head back against the wall. "If you ever decided to talk about this," he hisses, "we'd have to teach you a lesson. You wouldn't like it, take my word for it." His grip on my chin gets tighter and tighter.

I can't turn my head but I can see from the corner of my eye; the one called Butch spreads out my display panels on the floor. "Ain't this the sweetest show and tell you ever seen. Cute little puppies and kitties and everything."

Brenda Chitwood is spray painting black swastikas on my display. It seems so desperately cruel I start to sob. "Let's give her a little show and tell of our own," she says. "Let's pants the bitch."

They lift me up under the arms and by the ankles and start carrying me to the door to the back parking lot. I want to scream; but I don't have a voice. My head is splitting with a pain so bad it feels my eyeballs are spinning in their sockets. I don't know what they will do to me, but I have no power to resist. My bones have turned to liquid and every part of me is shaking.

Outside the door, they have me in a secluded niche of the parking lot. I watch their hands unfasten my jeans and start pulling them off.

The furious gray clouds are spinning in motion, faster and faster, like a pinwheel. *What further proof do you need? Have we not told you? Have we not told you again and again?*

Their hands are pulling my jeans roughly over my ankles. Are they going to take off my underpants as well? *Are they going to rape me with their huge, rigid organs? Will I be split up the middle like a seam?*

69

But something has suddenly launched me past the fear, into a different plane. It is truly remarkable. All of this is happening to someone else and I am merely watching. The sky is spinning so fast it seems motionless, like a whirling airplane propellor.

There is a hand tearing at my underpants and I feel the waistband cut into my side. Now I am dropped, I think, onto the blacktop. I think the Surly People are gone, but I have no idea why. I am numb in a zone I have never known. The whole world itself is enveloped in the mist. It is breathtaking, but where would I ever find words to describe it to anyone?

Miss Shapiro appears above me. She is like a spirit, suspended in the mist, but I still recognize her.

"Grace, what on earth? Are you hurt?"

"There appeared before me a multitude of the heavenly host, spinning prophecy to me in the voice of the angry clouds." My words come out flat like a chant, but are they even my words?

"I think there's a blanket in my car. We have to do something. Let me help you back into your clothes." She helps the white legs back into the blue jeans; the legs must belong to me.

"Miss Shapiro, look around you. It takes your breath away."

"Grace, I don't know what you mean."

"The transformation. Can you not see it?"

"Let's get you to my office. Do you think you can walk? Maybe the nurse is still here."

*

Mr. MacFarlane too is shrouded by the mist. He is saying, "I think you should take this matter up with the police, Mrs. Braun."

"Of course we'll take it up with the police," says my mother. "But right now, I intend to take it up with you."

Their voices are thin. I think some time has passed, but time has no meaning.

70

"When Grace gets her composure back, I'm sure she can tell us who is responsible for this."

"I'm sure she can too, but that's not the issue. What I'm saying to you is, I want to bring Grace here on my way to school. Every morning."

"Mrs. Braun, our policy is that students don't enter the building until eight o'clock A.M."

My mother has tears in her eyes. "I don't give a damn about your policy. Grace is in danger from these people, and I expect you to make some kind of adjustment."

"I can understand how upset you must be."

"Don't you patronize me. What I need from you is a little imagination. There has to be someplace she can wait. The office, the cafeteria, one of the study halls, *some*place."

Mr. MacFarlane says, "I suppose we could work something out."

"Thank you very much," says my mother. She turns to me. "Will this help you, Grace? Will it make you feel any safer?"

"I know what place this is," I say. The flat voice must belong to me; it only stands to reason. "This is Miss Shapiro's office."

"Please, Grace."

"It doesn't matter, I can assure you of that. The truth has been revealed to me. A transformation has taken place. If you look around you, do you not see it?"

"Please, Grace, don't talk this way."

"Father has gone to a different plane, but he is not dead. He speaks to me from the other side, in a sky voice. The Surly People are the agents of the forces of darkness. They have central organization but they are good at concealing it."

"Please." There are tears filling her eyes again.

"At all times and everywhere there are the forces of darkness and the forces of light, locked in combat. Father comes to me from the sky; he comes from the light. I have to be joined with the forces of

71

light. My part may even be an important one, but that too will be revealed to me. This is my time of preparation. The strength I need will be imparted to me."

"We need to talk to Dr. Rowe."

Four

I KEEP MY cookie under my pillow. Nobody knows it's there but me. In the looney bin, where everybody knows so much about you, even what you eat and if you wet the bed, it's nice to have a secret. Even if it's a small one.

I think the cookie's been there a long time, but I don't know how long. Yesterday and yesterday and yesterday, which day comes and which day goes? If Mrs. Grant tells me it's Friday, I trust her and believe her. As for finding my destinations, there is always the colored tape.

Mrs. Grant is standing in the mist. She floats above the floor like a wraith. But could you have a chubby wraith? I think she must have a special fondness for bowling. It would be rewarding to be on a bowling team; there would be togetherness and companionship and sisterhood.

Actually, the cookie is remarkable. I check on it from time to time; it crumbles at the edges, but it doesn't break. I would like to eat it but it's dry and brittle; I can't manufacture enough saliva.

I think my mother has been here to visit me today, but I can't be sure. My metal statue is here in my room, so it must be that she's been here to visit me.

Every night at supper, Mrs. Higgins makes me eat my Jell-O. Sometimes there are grapes in it, or grapefruit sections, or peach slices. I suppose I could survive forever on Jell-O and nothing but. I suppose anyone could. Jell-O with nuts, or raisins, or shredded

73

carrots, Jell-O with chopped celery, or pears, there's almost no limit to the possibilities.

But it takes a lot of saliva to eat a cookie. The cookie is large in circumference, but extremely thin. It is chocolate chip, but it also has M&Ms baked in it. Since it doesn't break, it must be that my head doesn't weigh very much. Of course it could also be that my head is actually quite heavy, but the pillow is an effective cushion.

Some days I talk to Dr. Rowe, but I can't remember what we say to each other.

I don't like to go to sleep at night. I like to sit in the lounge by the open window and listen to the mourning dove and hear the cattle lowing at the university farm at milking time.

"Grace, it's time for your medicine, and you need to get dressed."

Mrs. Grant means well, and she has my best interests at heart, but she is often in the mist. I say to her, "Mrs. Grant, floating in the mist must be disorienting for you."

"There's no mist here, Grace. Did you hear what I said to you?"

There is a farm report on television. Miss Ivey is sitting in her usual chair in front of the set. I wonder if anything she watches penetrates her brain.

Mrs. Grant takes a seat beside me.

"Mrs. Grant, if you'll be very, very still, there's a good chance you will hear the mourning dove."

"At least you know who I am today. I like mourning doves too, but you're not listening to what I'm telling you."

"No bird could ever be more precious to humanity than a dove, Mrs. Grant. Throughout the ages, the dove has stood for peace and harmony and healing. Even at the baptism of Jesus Christ, the Holy Spirit descended in the form of a dove."

She just says something more about getting cleaned up. Her

74

voice is beginning to pop with static. She is making a pest of herself. I suddenly feel cold, and start to quiver. I say to her, "If I'm clean enough, Mrs. Grant, will I get well?"

"That's not the point, Grace. Why are you shaking?"

"It's the static and the mist. It gives me the chills."

"There's no mist and no static either."

"Maybe if I scrubbed and scrubbed, I would be cleansed and purified. With thick, shiny hair, and lots of deodorant and baby powder and manicured, oval fingernails, and a transformation would take place. I would be in control." I am shivering and my teeth are chattering; I am giggling, or it might be sobbing, I'm not sure. I'm so glad Mrs. Grant is here.

*

Dr. Phyllis Rowe asks me about my metal sculpture.

"My father made it. It is made of old metal scraps, welded together. Beauty is painted with bronze-colored spray paint, but not the Beast. I wonder if he had it to do over again, if he would paint the Beast too."

"Maybe he thought it was appropriate for Beauty to be shiny and the Beast to be rusty."

It seems like a keen observation. I like it when she talks to me like this. I say, "I think you've hit the nail on the head. I think that's it exactly."

She says, "It's a lovely skill to take discarded materials and turn them into something beautiful."

Dr. Rowe is in her fifties, but quite attractive. Her long hair is grayish blond; when she was younger she was probably chic, like Miss Braverman. I say to her suddenly, "Dr. Rowe, I think I'd like to stay here." There are tears stinging my eyes; I don't know from whence they came or how fast.

75

"This is a hospital, Grace. People don't come to hospitals to stay, they come to get better."

"I'd like to stay here forever."

"Nobody stays here forever. If they don't get better, they go to a long-term facility." Her voice is starting to crackle with static; she is shorting out.

"I would like to stay here, it's so far from the world that hurts and scares."

"Not as far as it seems. A hospital is not as safe as it seems and the real world is not as scary as it seems."

"I love to sit at the open window in the lounge, in the early morning when it's so peaceful and quiet. I listen to the mourning dove and the cattle lowing at the farm at milking time. The dove is the sky and the farm is the earth. When you have the earth and the sky, you have the mother and the father; you have the ultimate meaning of life."

"If all your experience came through the window of an institution, I don't think you'd have much of life at all."

Her voice is full of static. If she insists on quarreling with everything I say, I'm going to get scrambled. I don't want to get scrambled, I have to change the subject. "Do you think if I loved my statue enough, it would come to life?"

"I don't understand what you mean." She pauses and lights a cigarette. Her lighter is pale gold and her fingernail polish is beige.

"Like the Pygmalion story from the Greeks. He sculpted a statue of a woman and he loved the statue so dearly that a goddess intervened and the statue came to life. If I loved the statue enough, do you think it might come to life?"

"It makes a good story, but I've never seen a statue come to life. I've seen people dead inside come to life, though."

"Dr. Rowe, please don't be offended, but why do you smoke cigarettes?"

76

"It's an old habit. I often think of quitting, but I never seem to get the job done. Maybe I don't have enough character. If the smoke bothers you, I'll put it out."

"No, please, it doesn't bother me. Besides, if you smoke cigarettes, it shows you're not perfect. Everyone's life is so sound except mine." People who are in control form a line in my brain. DeeDee. Miss Braverman. My mother. Dr. Rowe. Even the Surly People, because they live on such a primitive level, don't get scrambled or go flat out.

Dr. Rowe says, "Very few people are as much in control as they seem."

The tears are forming in my eyes again, and once again I blink them back. I don't want to cry and I don't want to get scrambled. "Dr. Rowe, would you have tea with me sometime?"

"How do you mean?"

"I'd like to have tea, just the two of us. We could have it with milk, if you like it that way. We could have some little biscuits and scones, like the English do."

"Do you mean here, when we're having one of our conferences?"

"Oh no, it would have to be a completely different environment, a tearoom or a parlor. And we couldn't talk about my psyche, or things that have to do with a pathological mind. We would talk about art and literature and current events."

"I think that sounds nice, Grace. You're an interesting person to talk to. I think I would enjoy it."

Her static is gone. I feel several moments of inner peace, even though the tears are rolling down my cheeks.

*

This is a different day, that much I'm sure of. If my dad comes today, we will probably read some Eliot. It's been so long since we read any of the cat poems.

77

Miss Ivey is in front of the set again, gripping her vibrating wrist. The television is so annoying. We got the cookies on Miss Ivey's birthday, and mine is still intact, beneath my pillow, with a tiny spot of wax in the center where the birthday candle burned down. Miss Ivey didn't know it was her birthday. She is a catatonic crone. Some day, many years from now, I will also be a catatonic crone.

I say this to Mrs. Grant and she says, "Nonsense. You will never be any such thing."

"How long will Miss Ivey stay here? Won't they have to find a special place for her?"

"I don't know, Grace. It's a decision I don't have to make, thank the Good Lord."

"Some day, I will be just like her. It's the only prognosis for my life which stands to reason. When I first knew it, it seemed like such a desperate thought, but not anymore. I think Miss Ivey is in a safe, peaceful zone where no pain or fear or desperation can ever reach her."

"That's not living, though."

"Even if you're right, what's so great about living?"

"I don't want to hear that kind of talk. Go get your shoes on; it's time for bowling."

"I don't want to go bowling."

"You don't have a choice. Your whole group is going."

"Why should I have to go bowling if I hate it?"

"You know why. Because your group voted to go."

"But I didn't vote to go."

"It makes no difference. Your group voted to go, and you go with your group. Now up and at 'em."

We go bowling.

We ride in the hospital van. The sky voice comes: *Bowling Alleys*

78

are places where Surly People congregate. The forces of darkness may be in your presence.

Please don't bother me right now.

Don't shrink from your mission. You stand in the legion of light.

Please go away from me; I never know what to do.

We arrive at the bowling alley, on the interstate. There are many people inside and they stare at us. Why shouldn't they? We don't belong here. Bowling and other sports are for people who are in control and whose lives are sound. It's absurd for us to come here and pretend. When you're crazy in the hospital, you pretend and pretend, as if you can be cured, the way a person with an infection can be cured with penicillin.

Mrs. Grant forces me to wear ugly bowling shoes. She enters our names on a computer screen suspended from the ceiling. Everywhere there are the staring eyes. I hate being this much in touch; just enough to feel disoriented and afraid and humiliated. It would be so much better to be in Miss Ivey's zone. Her world is safe; it can't be penetrated. It would be better to slide peacefully into the crimson water and sleep the sleep that never ends.

There is a new member of our group. He is called Luke. I never saw him before yesterday, but he is clearly one of the Surly People. He is on lockup, so a guard is supervising him here. Sometimes I have seen him playing Frisbee in the courtyard with his lockup guard.

His every movement is reckless. He launches his bowling ball down the shiny blond lane with such velocity that it scatters the pins in a shattering collision. He would love to smash the pins to bits.

He leaves our lane and sits with other Surly People in the next lane. He drinks some of their beer and they all smoke cigarettes and laugh loudly. Does he know them, or is there just some

79

brotherhood that connects Surly People wherever they meet? His security guard brings him back and tells him he will have to stay with the group.

"Whatever you say, Chief."

He comes close to me to sit, but I mustn't look at him. I must never look in his eyes. My heart pounds with fear and I look away. Suddenly, the memory of being molested by the Surly People is so vivid it brings tears to my eyes. I want to go to the bathroom.

Semper fidelis; this is the time to be on guard.

Please let me alone; I don't understand what you expect from me.

When my turn comes, I am still blinking back the tears; I feel so shaken I want to be skipped.

"Mrs. Grant, please go on to the next person. I just can't do it right now."

"Sure you can, Grace. All you have to do is roll a bowling ball. And while you're at it, you might try and have a little fun."

Her voice is crackling and I'm short of breath. "Mrs. Grant, I'll eat everything on my plate, I promise. Anything that's not flesh, I mean."

"Don't be silly. Take your turn and try to relax."

I am standing holding the ball. It is so very, very heavy my arms start to tremble. The bowling lane is pitched like the ridge of a roof or a mountain peak — if I don't throw the ball precisely down the sharp crease at the center, it will probably roll all the way down to the sea.

I know that people are staring at me. A thousand eyes, a thousand contemptuous eyes. My whole body is shaking and I can't hold back the tears. I move forward a step or two and drop the ball feebly to the floor with a thud. It rolls slowly into the gutter and then trickles forward about twenty feet. It comes to a dead stop. I am frozen in place, short of breath and quivering, staring at the motionless ball. The flashbulbs are popping in my brain.

80

There's no telling how much time passes, but it feels like forever. There are bursts of laughter from the nearby Surly People. A repeated beeping is coming from the computer screen above our lane; it is the eye. Even the darkest corner of my brain can't hide from the eye. It beeps again and again, carving in my brain.

No one dares to approach the ball; it is forbidden to walk down a bowling lane. There is only the repeated beeping. I am scrambled.

Then the one called Luke saunters down the lane and picks up the ball. He is total nonchalance and total contempt; a cigarette dangles from his lips. He launches the ball the rest of the way. It shatters the pins like a peal of thunder. On his way back he passes close to me; he smells of tobacco and a familiar after-shave. He is like all Surly People; there is nothing in life he respects and nothing can intimidate him.

I mustn't look in his eyes. His arm brushes my arm and I am chilled, covered with gooseflesh. I am shaking so that I can't turn to the right or the left. I will wet my pants and there will be a puddle beneath me, on the shiny blond floor.

He calls to Mrs. Grant, "What the hell, give her a strike." His voice is a hailstorm of static as he disappears into the mist.

"Mrs. Grant, can you help me please?"

"What is it, Grace? Turn around please."

"Can you help me down, Mrs. Grant? Can you help me down from the ridge? Please, I need to find the bathroom."

*

Dr. Rowe wants to know how I'm feeling.

"I am very, very sick. In plain language, I'm a schizophrenic."

"Schizophrenia is not plain language. I think you're more in touch."

"In touch is hospital talk," I say. "I'm in touch enough to be

81

frightened and get scrambled. But I'm very sick. I'm not going to get better."

She smiles at me. "A few days ago, you told me you didn't want to get better. You said you'd rather stay in the hospital."

"I can't see where the humor lies. My future is over; I'm going to spend the rest of my life one foot in the looney bin and one foot out."

"I wasn't making fun of you, Grace, lighten up."

"I see the schizophrenics every day. I study their details. Schizophrenia means your life is over. I'd like to hear you deny that I have it."

She says, "Since I can't think of a better name for it, we'll go ahead and call it a schizophrenic episode. But it is an *episode*. I'll tell you what I've told you before: I've seen many people recover from such episodes and live completely normal lives. I've never told you a lie, have I? Can you trust what I'm telling you?"

I have to listen to all this through the static. I don't know why she talks to me like a little child. "I would like very much to trust you," I say.

"You are more in touch, whether you like the phrase or not. You've been here for two weeks, do you realize that?"

"The time has no meaning. There are the days and nights. Mrs. Grant tells me the days and I take her word for it."

"Has your voice spoken to you lately?"

"My preparation is not yet complete. The sky voice warns me of the one called Luke."

"Does the sky voice speak as your father?"

"It is my father's voice. The light comes from above, from the other side. I think the eye and the voice are one."

"And who is Luke?"

"You already know him. He's a new patient."

"I know who you mean. Actually, he's not new to the hospital, but he's new to your group."

"If you say so. I would never tell you how to do your job, but could you please move him to a different group?"

"Why?"

"The sky gives me warnings about him. I wonder if I've ever told you about the train?"

"Yes, you have. What warnings?"

"The one called Luke is one of the Surly People."

"Nonsense. He is a patient here. It's that simple."

The static pops in her voice and a flashbulb breaks in my brain. I say, "The truth is, I don't want to be in a group. I hate it when they want me to talk in group. Would it be okay if I just worked on crafts instead?"

"We can't do it that way, Grace. If you're in our program, you're a member of a group. If there's more to tell about the warnings though, I would like to hear it."

"The sky warns me of him. He is one of the Surly People, and it's no accident that he is here. It's important for me to keep away from him; can you please move him to a different group?"

She shakes her head. "You're suggesting that there's a link between Luke and the hoodlums who assaulted you."

"Not only that but linked also to the evil that permeates the world at all times and everywhere."

She goes on, "Grace, let's get the sheep separated from the goats. What those hoodlums did to you was very cruel, but it wasn't part of anything that is organized. That event had nothing to do with any person, other than yourself, in this hospital."

Her voice is shorting out, I can't get all the words. She is lecturing me, which I probably deserve, but it makes me feel unworthy. Suddenly, the memory of the Surly People in the hallway is so strong I feel my bones have turned to pudding. The tears are blurring my eyes. The one called DeWayne with his seared eyebrow and his hot breath and the way he tore at my underpants with his horny fingers. It's safer with Dr. Rowe, but I think I've told her too much. The sky won't like it.

"One of them had arrows shaved in his head," I say. "They sprayed swastikas on my science project. They tore at my underwear, I hope they didn't rape me." Now the tears are rolling down my cheeks. Dr. Rowe hands me the box of Kleenex.

She says, "According to our examination, you were not raped, but it was a horrible thing they did to you."

"Why do they persecute me, Dr. Rowe? Where does such cruelty come from?"

"I'm not sure there's an easy answer for that. Sometimes people are very cruel."

The sky won't like that answer. I could tell her so, but she would just dismiss it. I wipe some of the tears which are still flowing, but at least I'm not sobbing. "I don't know why anyone would want to rape me," I say. "I'm not much to look at."

Dr. Rowe smiles at me. "I think you're attractive. You would probably be more attractive if you took more interest in your personal appearance."

I think for a moment of the hand clutching at the waistband of my underpants; I can't imagine what advantage there could be in being more attractive. "Dr. Rowe, are you going to lecture me about shaving my armpits and taking better care of my complexion?"

"I'd rather not lecture you about anything. I hope you don't perceive me that way."

I think suddenly of DeeDee's skin and her shining hair. "My friend DeeDee is very beautiful."

"I thought you told me you don't have any friends."

"DeeDee is the most open person. She has so much trust. I think she actually likes me."

"Why should it surprise you if someone likes you?"

84

"Or she did, anyway, before all of this. She feeds the fish in her underwear. Her skin is so tan and smooth. Sometimes I feel like touching her and holding my arms around her. Is it okay for me to have that feeling?"

"I don't know why not."

"You don't think I'm becoming a lesbian, do you?"

"Of course not."

Her words give me some relief. Dr. Rowe is very perceptive about many things. I'm not sure she understands about the sky voice, but I won't bring it up again. Someday, maybe the two of us will go to tea, and we will talk. Maybe we could go to the Shakespeare festival first. It would be perfect, no doctor and no patient, just two women having tea and talking about *A Midsummer Night's Dream*.

She lights one of her cigarettes and blows a stream of smoke up at the ceiling. The sockets of her eyes are dark. I wonder if she knows how to blow smoke rings. I've been told my Uncle Larry was very good at blowing smoke rings, but it would be completely inappropriate for a psychiatrist to blow smoke rings in her office. She wouldn't blow smoke rings at tea, either.

Five

Mrs. YOUNGBLOOD HAS put the one called Luke in the chair next to me. It makes me very tense. I sit very straight and still with my eyes down. There are lots of chairs available, it seems so unfair.

A patient called Professor Sarbanes is doing most of the talking. He is impatient and irritable and quite electrical.

It frightens me when we have group. I don't want to speak and I don't want to listen to these hopeless stories of lives that don't work. As crazy wild as I am, it could become even worse, and the thought fills me with fresh panic.

Mrs. Youngblood has turned to me. She is speaking to me.

"Did you hear me, Grace?"

Oh please no. I sit up even straighter.

"Grace, the group would like to hear from you."

"What group?" asks the one called Luke. "You're the only one askin' the questions." He is so near to me, I mustn't look at him. What meaning his remark holds, I do not know. My breath is coming short and the panic is rising in my stomach; I can't let myself get scrambled.

Mrs. Youngblood ignores Luke's remark. She says, "Recently, Grace suffered a very traumatic experience at her school. She was molested by a gang of hoodlums. Grace, would you like to tell the group about it?"

"Please no."

Mrs. Youngblood smiles. "I'm not sure we know exactly what *please no* means."

"Please, Mrs. Youngblood, I'd rather not talk about it."

"I'm sure part of you feels that way, but you might be surprised how talking about it would make you feel better."

I keep my eyes down. "I'd just rather not, please. I've talked to Dr. Rowe about it."

"I'm glad to hear that you've talked to Dr. Rowe about it, but you're also a member of this group, and that membership carries some responsibility."

Why can't she let me alone? "Please no," I say again.

The one called Luke lights a Marlboro and says, "I get the impression she doesn't want to talk about it."

Mrs. Youngblood says, "I appreciate your observation, Luke, but what Grace wants to do and what is good for her, may be two different things entirely. And let me remind you that it's not your job to decide what's best for other patients."

He shrugs. "If you say so."

"Before we go any further with the group, Luke, don't you think it would be a good idea if you asked if your cigarette smoke bothers anybody?"

"I could care less if it bothers anybody."

"I'm afraid that's not a very responsible group attitude."

He sprawls back in his chair and blows out some smoke. I watch him from the corner of my eye. His dark hair is long and curly, nearly to his shoulders. He wears a red and blue headband. He says to Mrs. Youngblood, "So kick me out. I don't want to be here anyway."

"How do you get the cigarettes, Luke?" she asks.

"I buy them."

"How?"

87

"With money."

"Am I supposed to think that's funny?"

"Does it look like I give a shit what you think?"

"Stores aren't supposed to sell cigarettes to minors," she says. "Where do you get them?"

"I have a secret supplier; a contact from Colombia. Why don't you get real?"

I can't comprehend the scope of his insolence. Is there nothing in heaven and earth that the Surly People fear or hold in respect?

Professor Sarbanes is irritated and impatient. He says to Mrs. Youngblood, "Will you please tell me, what is the point of this quibbling about cigarettes?"

I can see the anger rising in Mrs. Youngblood. She says to Professor Sarbanes, "Would you like to take over this group?"

"What I'd like to do, as long as we have to be here, is talk about something more important than the policy of stores selling cigarettes to minors."

Mrs. Youngblood glares at him and then turns back to me. She hasn't forgotten. She is a little more composed but her eyes are still bright with anger. Like ice. I can't understand the anger; it confuses me.

"Grace," she says, "the group is still waiting to hear from you."

"Please, Mrs. Youngblood, can you please move on to someone else?" My tears are like a torrent.

She says, "Grace, try to stop crying."

I reach for the tissues. I can't speak.

"Did you hear me, Grace? All these tears are not necessary."

"Mrs. Youngblood, you have too much static. I'm afraid I'm going to get scrambled. I get so confused."

"Wipe your eyes and blow your nose, Grace. You'll feel a lot better. We'll let you off the hook today, but sooner or later you'll have to share with the group."

88

I start wiping my face. The one called Luke says to me, "I don't know what the punks did to you, but if they ever try it again, give 'em a kick in the nuts."

I look at him and our eyes meet. It feels as though his eyes are piercing my whole brain and right on out through the back of my head. *He can look clear through me.* I want to look away but I don't. Why is he so clean, even his fingernails are clean. It's not consistent with the way of the Surly People. Is he giving me advice? The sky would warn that he is setting a very subtle trap. I don't always listen to the sky the way I should. It's very confusing and I still have tears on my face.

"I don't understand you," I say.

"My advice is, a shot to the gonads. You'd be amazed how quick the fight goes out of 'em."

I turn away quickly and blow my nose. His eyes have chilled me. "You made Mrs. Youngblood mad," I say. "You caused her anger."

"I can't make her do anything. That's her problem."

In a stern voice Mrs. Youngblood says, "Is that the way you solve your problems, Luke? A kick in the groin?"

"You know a better way?"

Mrs. Youngblood ignores his question. She opens a folder and begins to leaf through it. "Since you're a new member of this group, Luke, maybe you'd like to tell us a little something about yourself."

"You've got the folder, why don't you save me the trouble?"

She is still studying the folder. "It seems to me you don't learn very much from experience."

"The way they usually tell me, is that I'm unsocialized. Whatever that means."

"Maybe you'd like to tell the group why you're here in the first place."

He lights another Marlboro. "I was in the south wing lockup," he says. "Dr. Rowe decided I needed to be over here instead, so here I am."

"Why were you on lockup?" asks Mrs. Youngblood.

"I'm waitin' to go to trial for murder. A friend of mine was paralyzed in the hospital, so I pulled the plug on his respirator."

"You killed your friend?"

"Clean the wax out of your ears. I just told you I pulled his plug."

"You killed your friend, Luke. Let's talk plain. And I don't hear much remorse in your voice."

"You want me to lay on the floor and bawl like a baby? Would that make you feel better?"

"If this person is a murderer," says Professor Sarbanes, "why is he here with us?"

"Not so fast, please," says Mrs. Youngblood. "Luke, you caused the death of your friend. Do you feel remorse for what you did?"

"It's too bad, but he's better off dead. Lots better. He wanted to die."

"How do you know that?"

"He told me with blinks. He couldn't talk but he could blink for yes and no."

Someone asks, "Why was he in the hospital?"

"He was in a bike accident."

"Do you mean a motorcycle?"

"Yeah, man, a Harley. He skidded off the road on some bluff over by the Quad Cities. It didn't hurt the bike too much, but there was a lot of damage to John's spinal cord. He was paralyzed."

"So you took it upon yourself to be his executioner," says Mrs. Youngblood.

Luke shrugs. "What the hell, somebody had to do it. It was what he wanted. He couldn't pull his own plug, and the nurses sure as hell weren't going to do it for him."

"This person is a simple psychopath," says Professor Sarbanes to

Mrs. Youngblood. "If Dr. Rowe made the decision to put him in our group, I think it was poor judgment."

"We can talk about that later," says Mrs. Youngblood.

Professor Sarbanes is red in the face and beginning to twitch. He says, "She has put our safety in jeopardy, to put it bluntly. I'm going to make a formal complaint."

"That's your right," says Mrs. Youngblood. She turns back to Luke. "What if your friend had gotten better? What if his condition had improved?"

"He wasn't going to get any better."

"What makes you so sure?"

"The nurses told me. He was in the hospital a month when I first went to see him. He was a vegetable then, and that's all he was ever gonna be."

"It seems to me that you need to take a long, hard look at the way you make decisions," says Mrs. Youngblood.

"You must have me confused with someone else," says Luke.

"What do you mean by that?"

"You must have me confused with someone who gives a shit what you think or don't think. You're just a flat-out bullshitter, baby, and I don't pay no attention at all to bullshitters."

"What is a bullshitter, Luke? And don't you ever call me baby."

"A bullshitter is a person like you who runs the lives of people like me."

"You are a psychopath, young man," says Professor Sarbanes. He is scarlet in the face and trembling so, but he continues. "If you happen to come across patients in this hospital who say they want to die, and I can assure you that you will, are you going to kill them too?"

Luke grins at Professor Sarbanes and says, "Hey, that's a thought. Maybe I'll start with you." Then he throws back his head and laughs.

Professor Sarbanes wants to say something more, but he can't. He is trembling so furiously that he is practically vibrating. There is even a line of drool running down his chin. I feel so bad for him, I know the loss of control he feels.

All by himself, Luke has sabotaged the group. What is the source of this power for chaos?

*

On Tuesday morning, Mother visits me in my room. I hug her and cling to her. When I was little, she pulled me to her in the kitchen and her apron was dusted with flour and little scraps of bread dough were stuck to her fingers.

She has brought me some gazpacho in the mason jar. "I'll get Mrs. Higgins to okay this," I say. "When food comes from the outside, it has to be okayed. Last night the menu was chicken, and Mrs. Higgins made me some rice pilaf. I think she brought it from home."

"That was nice of her," my mother says. "Did you eat it?"

"A little bit. My appetite is somewhat better."

She has also brought me the Looney Tunes tee shirt and Uncle Larry's fatigue jacket. They are both freshly laundered with the clean smell.

"It seems much too warm to wear a fatigue jacket," she says.

"I need to have it though. I get so chilled sometimes."

Then my mother asks me for the names of the people who molested me.

"Please don't ask me that, Mother. Let's just have a nice talk."

"I have to ask you. Mr. MacFarlane needs to know and so do the police."

"You mustn't ask me this question. I've told you."

"You know their names, Grace. Please tell me. If they're allowed to get away with this, they'll just continue to trample on the rights of other people."

92

"Please let's talk about something else."

"They have to understand that their actions have consequences. People like that don't learn any other way."

My eyes are suddenly blurred by tears. "They told me if I ever told, I would regret it. There's no telling what horrid thing they might do to me."

The tears are streaming down my face and my mother holds me. I say, "They told me they would teach me a lesson. God, who do these people think they are? What useful lesson could they ever teach anybody?"

"I know it won't be easy for you," she says. "I know that, believe me. But I think I've worked out protection for you. You can ride to school with me in the mornings. Mr. MacFarlane will let you enter the building early. After school, you can stay in Miss Braverman's room until I pick you up. I've okayed it with her."

I pull myself loose and sit on my bed. I wipe my eyes and blow my nose. "I still have my cookie," I say.

"What cookie?"

"We got them on Miss Ivey's birthday. Mine is safe under my pillow. When my appetite is back, I'll probably eat it."

"Please, Grace, don't do this."

"I wonder how long a cookie could last before it underwent total disintegration. A year? Five years? A thousand years? How long would it take until it was broken down into its tiniest molecular parts and atoms?"

"We're not talking about cookies."

"I don't want to stay in Miss Braverman's room. I have lots of respect for her, but it seems so desperate because it's artificial."

"I see your point, but it wouldn't have to be forever, just till you feel comfortable."

"I'd rather walk home with DeeDee and feed the fish and fertilize her ornamental trees."

"That might be nice, but you'd have to talk to DeeDee about it."

"Do you think she'll still want to be my friend, even after all of this? How long can you be crazy wild and still keep a friend?"

"I'm sure she'll still be your friend. She called two or three times to ask how you're doing."

"She hasn't called me, though."

"Only because I told her not to; I was afraid it might be embarrassing for you."

Mother is probably right; it *would* be embarrassing. "You know what, Mother? The truth is, according to Dr. Rowe, I need to be more like you. I need to do what you did."

"What did I do?"

"After Dad died, you went out and finished your education and started a career. You stopped living in his shadow and became independent. You became your own person."

"Is that how Dr. Rowe sees it? I didn't know the two of you talked so much about me."

"That's how she sees it. She says the two things that paralyze me are over now. My dad is gone, and my mother has stopped withdrawing."

"Withdrawing?"

"Please don't feel bad, this is just the way Dr. Rowe and I talk about things. Dad was so intense and such an activist, and deep down inside I thought you were withdrawing, like sort of withdrawing from a battle. I didn't know these things in my conscious mind, though, they were happening in my unconscious."

My mother's eyes are bright with tears. She says, "Maybe I *was* withdrawing; I never thought of it like that. I only thought I was doing the things I knew how to do. I never had much confidence, you know."

"You mustn't feel bad, Mother, and you mustn't feel guilty. Dr. Rowe says it's mostly my own doing. I was withdrawn to begin

94

with, and then I looked at my parents and I withdrew even from myself. I am split off from myself."

"These are such deep thoughts," she says. "They go right over my head."

"No offense, Mother, but that's what I'm talking about. You're doing it right now. Would you like to have my cookie? I'll be happy to give it to you."

"I don't think so. Thank you anyway."

"It might as well go to someone who can use it. Do you know what, Mother? I think I'd like to go home."

"Grace, I'd love to have you home, but you can't leave the hospital until Dr. Rowe says so."

"You can talk to her. You see how much I've learned, you can tell her that."

"But Grace, I don't understand. The last time I was here you wanted to stay in the hospital."

"That was then, and this is now. Please don't speak with all that static. Dr. Rowe has taught me much, and I've learned it. I am even ignoring the sky voice, at least most of the time."

"Grace, I'm confused. I don't know what's best." A tear is sliding down her cheek. I sit beside her and hold her hand and my eyes are blurry again.

"Mother, one of the Surly People is here in the hospital. He sits next to me in group."

"You mean one of the people who molested you is *here?*"

"No, but don't forget the link that connects all Surly People. Except for the fact that he has so much hygiene, he is essentially one of them."

"I'm confused about a lot of things, Grace, but I'm sure that's not a good way for you to think. Dr. Rowe has probably told you the same thing."

"I've learned the basic truth from Dr. Rowe; that's what I'm trying to tell you. I don't know why Mrs. Youngblood forces me to sit next to him; there are plenty of other chairs he could sit in. As a matter of fact, I'm not absolutely sure Mrs. Youngblood can be trusted. I know how bizarre that must sound, but I really and truly mean it."

"Who is Mrs. Youngblood?"

"She's the therapist in our group. She lost her temper. The one called Luke caused her anger."

"Why is it so important that a woman loses her temper? We have to trust Dr. Rowe's judgment. She'll let us know when it's time for you to come home."

"Mother, I asked you politely about the static. I'm trying to tell you I need to come home. It frightens me to spend all this time with people who are this crazy. Professor Sarbanes believes his thought rays are heating the earth's core, and because of the overheating, the earth is going to explode."

"Grace, please. I'll talk to Dr. Rowe but that's all I can do."

She thinks she will hide behind her static. I am turning to stone and my voice is lifeless: "Mother, why don't you go home and bake bread?"

*

Mrs. Youngblood has put me next to the one called Luke Wolfe again. When I ask her to move me to a different seat, she says something about facing up to problems. I think the group will not go well today; already I sense the anger rising.

Mrs. Youngblood says, "I think Luke has something to report to the group this morning."

Luke lights a cigarette but doesn't speak.

"Luke has lost his TV privileges. Don't you think you ought to tell us how that happened, Luke?"

"It's a real boring story. I don't think anybody would be interested."

96

Mrs. Youngblood has the folder open. "I have to disagree with you, Luke. I think the group would find it very interesting. But what's even more important, I think it might do you some good to talk about it."

"You're just a flat-out bullshitter. What you're really into is your power trip."

Mrs. Youngblood is looking in the folder and smiling. "You've always had a problem with authority, haven't you?"

He blows out some smoke and says, "Some people seem to think so."

"And you? What do you think?"

"I think I'd like to have bullshitters like you off of my back and out of my life."

Professor Sarbanes interrupts and says irritably to Mrs. Youngblood, "Can you please get to the point? What is the point here?"

"We are waiting for Luke's report," she answers.

"That's all well and good, but maybe you could do something to speed things up a little bit."

"It would probably do you some good to take a few deep breaths and slow down a little," she says to Professor Sarbanes.

"You have no idea what is good for me," he answers. "My time on this earth is limited."

I can feel the knot constricting in my stomach; my breath is coming short. "Mrs. Youngblood, please," I say.

"What is it, Grace?"

"My sky voice is diminishing and Dr. Rowe has given me keen insight. But there is anger coming."

"Anger upsets you, doesn't it, Grace?"

"Please, it causes me to get scrambled. Try and ignore the static. In the air, hostility and confrontation are rigid."

"We'll try and keep everything on an even keel, Grace." She

97

turns again to Luke. "It seems there is some impatience in the group, Luke. Why don't you fill everybody in?"

He puts out his cigarette and says, "Yesterday, I dressed my roommate up before he went to crafts."

"What does that mean, you dressed him up?"

"I put a dust mask on his face. I put a motorcycle helmet on his head. I taped his fingers together with adhesive tape."

"Did you think it was cute to dress your roommate up in that fashion?"

"I thought it might keep the bullshitters off his back. He's always givin' the finger and stickin' things in his mouth and ears. The nurses are always on his case, but I don't think he can help what he does."

"Is that how you see it?"

"How I see it is, my roommate doesn't even belong here. He's a dodo. He belongs in some other kind of facility."

"A dodo?" says Mrs. Youngblood.

"Yeah, a dodo. A retard."

"Is that how you refer to mentally retarded people?"

"Yeah, dodos. It's not a put-down, I like dodos. I used to live with them, in one of the group homes I was in. I was even workin' in the dodo house cafeteria before I came here."

Mrs. Youngblood still has the folder open. "It says here, Luke, that your cafeteria job was another place where you had difficulty with authority."

"I've got a good idea," he says. "Why don't you take your folder and shove it up your ass?"

I feel I can't stand any more. I press my hands over my ears. I say suddenly, "Mrs. Youngblood, please. There's too much anger."

She turns to me with eyes that glitter. "Grace, do you have something to add to this conversation? Do you have a question for Luke?"

98

"You are in the mist and there is all the static. So much hostility frightens me, I'm getting scrambled."

"I think where you find Luke, you find anger. You know a lot about anger, don't you, Luke?"

"I know a lot about bullshitters and their power trips. What it comes down to is, they just can't stand it if the square pegs don't fit in the round holes."

"Was that the problem in your cafeteria job, Luke?"

"There wasn't any problem until the douche bag supervisor made one."

"I figured it would be something like that." Mrs. Youngblood smiles, but it is a smile without humor. "Why don't you tell us about it?"

"You'll probably wet your pants if I don't. The supervisor decided that all the boy dodos should stand at the urinal to take a leak. Their usual way was to sit on the pot and do it. She was afraid they were sittin' there and playin' with themselves instead of takin' a leak."

"What did it have to do with you?"

"Nothin'. She wanted me to help her enforce her new policy. I told her to kiss off; my job was in the cafeteria. Besides, I couldn't see anything wrong with it. The dodos don't get too many grins out of life, maybe they deserve a chance to jerk off every once in a while."

"What you're really telling this group is that when you caused your friend's death by pulling the plug on his respirator, you were acting in a way that is consistent with the rest of your behavior."

"I'm not tellin' this group anything, because they don't give a shit. The only one playin' the game is you."

"You just don't like anyone telling you what to do, do you?"

"Brilliant. You figured that out all by yourself. Maybe you ought to give yourself a gold star."

Six

MISS IVEY IS sitting in front of her test pattern but she is on the far side of the room and the noise doesn't disturb me. It is six A.M. The sky is lightening through the east window, but it is a gray dawn.

I have had a dream which has awakened me, but it wasn't a bad dream. It was lovely, it was a dream of my father; the two of us were walking across a huge meadow, and he had cut for me a cluster of the lovely white roses.

The mist is lifting from the lounge carpet like haze on a meadow at dawn. But there's no mist in the lounge, really. It was part of the dream of the meadow.

A gentle rain is falling. I can hear it dripping from the eaves. I feel calm as a tranquil pond. If only this moment could be locked in place with me inside it. There's a song called "Time in a Bottle." If only I could be fixed here, on this point in time, and the serenity would be everlasting unto everlasting. There would never be the disorienting hallways at school, or group therapy, or butchering of gentle farm animals, or Surly People, or any of the things which hurt and scare.

> *And the early morning dawn, it sleeps so peacefully,*
> *Soothed by long fingers.*

Through the open window I hear the cooing of the dove and the lowing cattle and the muffled, distant traffic.

"They got any coffee around here?"

The loud voice startles me. I look up and it is the one called Luke Wolfe. He struts at all times; is it the strut of a predator? My pulse quickens and my mouth turns dry. His hair is damp and I can smell his after-shave.

"What did you say, please?"

"I said is there any coffee around here?" His voice crackles with static and he is blocking the light from the east window, he is sort of like a silhouette.

"I don't think so," I say quickly. "In the cafeteria there is coffee for the staff, but I'm quite sure it's not meant for patients."

He leaves without a word, strutting down the west wing toward the cafeteria. I'm sure he would never need to consult the blue line or the yellow line or any of the lines. He won't come back here, surely. He won't want to be in the lounge at dawn. If he does come back, I will be all alone with him, except for Miss Ivey who doesn't really count, because she is here only in body. I feel the panic rising in my stomach. It would be much safer to go to my room, but I stay in my spot on the couch, hoping to remember the dream and recapture the peaceful moment.

He returns, with steaming coffee in a large Styrofoam cup.

"They gave you some," I say.

"I took some," he says. He is wearing a red tank top. He could break me with his heavy muscles. He sits at the card table and lights a cigarette.

For a few minutes he smokes his cigarette and drinks his coffee. My pulse will not slow down; I try to keep my mouth moist.

He finally breaks the silence. "So tell me. What is a psychopath?" He seems bored.

"Excuse me?"

"What is a psychopath? People keep callin' me a psychopath, and I don't know what the hell it means."

The nurses' station is only a few feet around the corner. If Mr. Sneed is there, he could help me.

"There's going to be anger," I blurt out. "Will there be anger?"

"Hey, man, don't come unglued. It's just a question. If you don't know the answer, that's cool." He gets up and strides across the room. He switches off Miss Ivey's television set. She seems to take no notice of him.

He returns to his chair and sits down. "Jesus Christ, a goddam test pattern."

I moisten my lips and my mouth. "A psychopath is a person without a conscience," I say quietly. "A person with a basic personality component that's missing."

"Is that it?"

He thinks I am finished, but I am only swallowing so I can go on. "A psychopath feels no remorse for the evil that he does. He hates to get caught, but he doesn't feel remorse for the deed itself."

He puffs on his cigarette but doesn't speak. He is folding his red and blue bandana tight into a band. I must be very careful of what I say. I have seen the anger of Surly People and I have seen his anger too. "You have to understand, I'm only trying to answer your question. I'm not calling you a psychopath."

"That's cool." He is knotting the headband into place around his head.

"Also, please remember I didn't make the definition, I'm just reporting it. There's much more to it than what I've told you. In the first floor lounge there's a library of psychology books. You could read up on it if you wanted to." It sounds like such an absurd suggestion. It's the fear that causes me to babble like this, why does the fear control everything?

"You sound real uptight," he says.

"I almost always am," I blurt out.

"So what are you in for?"

102

"I'm never sure. Just crazy wild, I guess. I've spent lots of time in looney bins, sometimes I think it's a life sentence. The years will pass and I will make lots of ashtrays and candy dishes. They used to call them ashtrays but now they call them candy dishes." It is the fear that makes me babble like this. I mustn't anger him but I mustn't tell him anything that's real. But do I even know what is real? I have seen him penetrate Mrs. Youngblood's sphere and I know he can penetrate mine. He is no accident.

"You talk funny," he says. He has lit a new cigarette. "That's one thing you notice about the puzzle house, people talk funny."

There are tears dimming my eyes, but I mustn't let him see me cry. Why did he have to disturb the peace of the lounge at dawn? Maybe Mrs. Grant will come early with the medicine.

"Please don't be offended," I say, "but did you truly kill your friend?"

"I pulled the plug on his respirator. It comes down to the same as killing him."

"Was it hard?"

"It wasn't a hard decision, if that's what you mean. I thought I was doin' him a favor. I know I was. He wanted to snuff and I couldn't blame him. Would you want to spend your whole life as a vegetable? There's worse things than death is how I look at it."

I think suddenly of the crimson water, warm and peaceful, and I blurt out, "It's so true. There are many things worse than death, such as a life of loneliness or fear or disorientation."

He looks at me with curiosity, then shrugs his shoulders. "Anyway, the only hard part was figurin' out how. I had to wait until the nurses were busy someplace else, then I had to open the console and cut a couple circuits."

"It must be that you are mechanically inclined," I say. It will be better if I can keep him talking about himself, and then Mrs. Grant will bring the medicine.

"A little," he says. "It wasn't the hairiest job in the world. Actually, according to my lawyer and my social worker, I'm not even supposed to be talkin' about this shit. I mean it's okay to talk about Johnny dyin', but I'm not supposed to talk about any of the details."

"I promise I would never breathe a word to a soul, please believe me."

He throws back his head and laughs, so harsh, the way he sometimes does in group. His teeth are straight and regular. "What the hell, they're just thinkin' about all the legal bullshit. I have to go to trial next month. They're afraid I'm gonna talk to newspaper reporters."

"Are they going to put you in jail?"

"It's possible. Anything's possible. They don't even know yet if I'm gonna have a bench trial or a jury trial or just a hearing. That's what I'm in here for. I have to have a total psych evaluation before I can go to trial. Somewhere out there in some air-conditioned conference room, a bunch of prime bullshitters will sit around and figure it all out."

"Please, what exactly is a bullshitter?"

He looks directly into my eyes. "Bullshitters are the lazy fatasses who sit around in expensive suits in big offices. They never do any real work, all they do is make decisions that control other peoples' lives. I've been in the social services system all my life. That means the government basically, and that's where you find the most bullshitters."

His dark eyes have locked me in like small, black mirrors and I can't look away. There is a tiny reflection of myself in both his eyes. What am I doing in his eyes? Am I teeny-tiny like Alice, that I can locate in his eyes?

I look away quickly and try for breath. "But what about your parents? Can they not help you?" I hurry to moisten my mouth.

"I never had any parents. I mean I never knew who they were. I've always been in group homes or foster homes."

"I'm sorry, I'm really so sorry. I didn't mean any harm."

"No sweat, that's ancient history. Is there any way you could cut down on all the apologies?"

"Please excuse me. I know something about ancient history, I take it at school. Mr. McCorkindale is my teacher. Miss Braverman is my science teacher. I'm not a good science student, but I'm very fond of her. Please excuse me, but when I'm stressed I get quite incoherent in my conversation. I believe it to be a defense mechanism to avoid getting scrambled. Dr. Rowe agrees with me."

"I never met anybody that talks like you do. I know McCorkindale, though. I had him for a class last year."

"We go to the same high school? You go to West High?"

He asks, "You go there? I never saw you."

"This is my first year. We just moved to town this summer."

"Yeah, that would explain it. It was about the first day of school that I was over in the Quad Cities pullin' Johnny's plug. I was only back in school for a few days and then the cops came."

"How did they know it was you who did it?"

"I didn't try to cover my tracks or anything, I was about the only visitor John ever had. It didn't take a genius to figure out who did it. Anyway, after the cops came, they put me in juvenile detention. Then they sent me here. One way or the other, I'm done with school. If I go to the slammer or if I don't, either way I'm not goin' back to school."

"But isn't this your senior year?"

"It depends how you look at it. If I went back I would be a senior, but I just told you I'm not goin' back."

"I have to repeat my sophomore year," I say. "I've spent too much time in mental institutions."

He puts out his cigarette and drinks a little of his coffee. "That's

105

what I'm tryin to tell you about bullshitters. Anyone could see, with your brains, that's a bullshit decision. But you had no say in it. Am I right?" I don't know what to say, so he changes the subject: "You've got a lot of red in your hair. I never noticed it. Anybody ever call you Red?"

I look quickly away. Has he been watching my hair? I am still frightened but I don't think there will be anger or violence with a conversation like this. "Not that I can remember," I say. "But I can tell you one thing. It doesn't help to have a high I.Q. if you get scrambled in your mind or if your brain gets whizzed up with data."

"I wouldn't know what that means, but you can't apologize for the decisions bullshitters make. That's like givin' 'em a transfusion."

"But please, if you don't go back to school, what will you do with your life?"

"I'll be out on my own, makin' my own way. All I want is to get free and clear, and find some kind of job that lets me go my own way with no bullshitter lookin' over my shoulder. I might drive a rig and roll on down the highway."

"I would never mean to be quarrelsome, but wouldn't it be easier for you if you got your diploma first?"

"Who needs a piece of paper? The secret to makin' your own way is keep your needs simple so you don't need a lot of money. I talked to this guy once who worked on boat repair in Boston Harbor. He didn't work on ocean liners, the boats were big sailboats and schooners, all owned by a very rich bullshitter who rented them out to other bullshitters for cruises. Anyway, the guy I talked to would work a while, then be off a while, dependin' on whether the boats needed repair or if he was short of cash. There are ways, believe me."

His self-assurance is so complete it intimidates me. I can't think of anything more to say, but it would be uncomfortable to sit with him in silence or look into his eyes.

106

A checkerboard and the pieces are on the card table. He asks me if I want to play a game. I think checkers is a very boring game, but I would never say that to him. He sets up the pieces and I sit across from him. I wonder if checkers is played anywhere other than mental institutions.

"I have my own rules for checkers," he says.

"Please, what does that mean?"

"The usual way is too boring. The way I play, when you get to the back row and get a king, you get to change the rules any way you want. You get to decide how all the pieces move. You can move them backwards, sideways, double, or anything you want."

He makes me very uncomfortable. If the rules are changed, it will be stressful. "It sounds so complicated," I say.

"Nah. Nothin' to it. Then if the other guy gets a king, he gets to change the rules any way *he* wants. It goes back and forth like that; the rules are always changin'."

"I get confused about things sometimes."

"You need to chill out a little bit. It's no sweat, just make a move. Any move you want."

We play for a few minutes, then Mrs. Grant comes. It's time for medicine, she says. I need to go to the bathroom, I have to pee so badly. I am relieved that she has come.

*

I have forced the last blob of grouting compound between the tiny blue and white squares of ceramic tile. The compound dries gritty on my fingers; this is the fourth candy dish I have made. I have no idea what my mother and I will do with four candy dishes, we never eat candy.

"Mrs. Meade," I say, "correct me if I'm wrong, but I think these used to be called ashtrays."

"That's correct."

"But when smoking became socially unacceptable, it seemed appropriate to change the name from ashtray to candy dish. Is that how the evolution occurred?"

"Something like that."

"I suppose I could call two of them ashtrays and the other two candy dishes, but what if you don't smoke cigarettes or eat candy either?"

"You'll just have to find some other use for them."

"It would be nice to bring Beauty and the Beast to crafts someday and spray paint the beast. Do you have gold spray paint? Of course I'm not sure my father meant it to be that way, and the paint would have to be a perfect match. I'll tell you what: it would be nice to make an *Ojo de Dios*."

"My, aren't we talkative today," says Mrs. Meade. "I'll tell *you* what. I'll bring some sticks and yarn tomorrow so you can make an *Ojo*."

"Thank you of course, Mrs. Meade, I'll be happy to work on one. But I have to keep in mind that eyes and voices in the sky are really delusional."

Mrs. Higgins comes in. She tells me I have visitors.

"Please, Mrs. Higgins, I don't understand."

"You have two visitors in first floor lounge. I've come to take you down."

"What about my raisin dish? I've decided to call it a raisin dish."

"You can come back to it. Come on now, Grace, let's go."

She leads the way down the hall while I follow. The knot forms in my stomach. "Mrs. Higgins, I've never had visitors before. Is it someone besides my mother?"

She smiles. "Why not wait and find out? Be surprised."

Be surprised? Is that what she said? "But who are the visitors? I hope they're not from the criminal justice system. The one called

108

Luke Wolfe told me some things about his crime the other day. But I didn't seek the information, I've done nothing wrong."

"Grace, please calm down. It's no one from the legal system; I think they're from your school."

When we get to the first-floor lounge, I stop and stare. It's DeeDee and Miss Braverman. They are sitting on the couch in the corner, beneath the shelves of library books.

A small corner of my mind is happy to see them, but the knot in my stomach constricts in shame and humiliation. For several moments I stand as stiff as a statue.

I finally walk over to them. "I've never had visitors before," I say. "I'm not sure what to do."

"Neither are we," says Miss Braverman. "We wanted to visit, but we didn't want to make you uncomfortable."

"I can see right away that it's nice to have visitors," I say. "But it's also humiliating. I'm not sure I want people to see me here. Do you understand what I'm trying to say, Mrs. Higgins?"

"Yes, I do understand. But just relax and have a nice visit. I'll be back in a little while."

After she leaves, I sit straight on the couch. DeeDee is wearing a yellow sundress; her arms and shoulders are golden brown. Miss Braverman's dress is aqua with stripes. I am keenly conscious of my own clumpy, unkempt appearance.

"We miss you at school," says Miss Braverman.

I think immediately of the hallways, so long and confusing, and some of them where danger lurks. There is only a trace of static in Miss Braverman's voice. "I'm sure I'm not going to cry, Miss Braverman, and I'm also sure I won't get scrambled. Please, you must forgive my appearance. I didn't know anyone was coming. I have my Looney Tunes tee shirt, but it's not clean at the moment."

"You look just fine, Grace."

"It would be nice to have a visit, but we must try to avoid long, awkward silences."

Miss Braverman smiles. "That's not likely to happen with DeeDee and me in the same room."

"How are you doing?" DeeDee wants to know.

"I come and go," I say quickly. "I have good days and bad. I always take my medicine, but I don't know if it helps me. Dr. Rowe helps me understand things; she has so much insight into the pathological psyche."

Miss Braverman asks, "Dr. Rowe is your doctor?"

"Not only mine, but everybody's. I wish I could talk to her more often, but there are so many crazy people."

"Is there anything you need from school?" DeeDee asks.

"No, thank you. My mother brings my homework. I have my dad's Beauty and the Beast sculpture, and I have a cookie which has gone far beyond its life expectancy."

DeeDee stands up. She says to Miss Braverman, "Should I get it now?"

"You might as well," Miss Braverman answers.

Their exchange confuses me. DeeDee leaves and Miss Braverman says to me, "We brought you something. We decided to leave it in the car until we were sure we'd get to see you."

"You brought me a surprise?"

"It's just a little something we thought you ought to have."

Suddenly, I feel a lump in my chest. "It's so thoughtful of you to bring me a surprise."

"Don't get your hopes too high, Grace. It's not a new Corvette or anything like that." Then she wants to know about the books on the shelves behind us.

"This is the library," I tell her. "These are all psych books and medical books about mental disorders."

"I'll bet you spend a lot of your time reading."

110

"Sometimes in the evening I sit here and read. Sometimes it's too scary. If you're sick, it's good to know about your illness. Dr. Rowe says knowing is good, but acting is better."

"If I had to guess, I'd say you've been a book reader most of your life."

"It's true I've always been a bookworm. It's my father's influence. When I was small, we read together just about every folk and fairy tale there ever was. But there's probably a bad side to it. Instead of relating to other people, I've always been alone with a book. I like reading, but it's also a way for me to withdraw. Things scare me, so I withdraw. I don't mean to talk so much, but isn't it amazing how everything seems to have its good side and its bad side." I can't imagine I'm making any sense, I'm not calm, but Miss Braverman says, "That's a good point."

"Miss Braverman, at least I could have done something with my hair. Nice hair is a nice thing. Do you use a conditioner on your hair? I think it would be really good for me to take more care with my appearance."

She laughs. "Stop worrying about your appearance. You look just fine. Yes, I use a conditioner. When you shampoo your hair every day, it's supposed to be healthy to use a conditioner."

"Shampooing one's hair every day is such a lofty thought. But that's probably what I should do. That's probably the way life is meant to be lived; there would be so much control that way."

Then DeeDee returns. She has a very large rectangle under her arm, wrapped in brown paper.

"Surprise, Grace," she says. She stands the rectangle up on the couch and begins to tear away the wrapping.

It is my science project. DeeDee separates all four panels so that they are standing side by side.

"It's my science project," I say dumbly. "But it's not defaced."

"Take a closer look," says Miss Braverman. "Go ahead."

111

I get up to stand right in front of the panels. I can see that the posters have traces of white markings. Some of the white is a slightly different color. But the lettering and the pictures are clear, with no swastikas.

I say, "I don't understand."

"DeeDee repaired your project," explains Miss Braverman. "She fixed it. It got a rating of excellent, which means you can enter it in the regional science fair at Northwestern."

Immediately, my eyes are blurred with tears. "DeeDee, how did you do this? How did you fix it?"

"If there was enough room, I used poster paint. For the tight spots, mostly around the lettering, I used typewriter whiteout." Her eyes are sparkling.

"It must have been so much work for you."

"It didn't seem like a lot of work. I felt so bad about what happened to you."

"I can't tell you how kind and thoughtful it is," I say. I have tears sliding down my face. "DeeDee, please, I'd like to give you a hug now."

We hold each other. Her slick, cool shoulders. Her hair smells fresh and sweet. "It's so kind and thoughtful of you," I say again. "My mother said you would still be my friend, but I just can't imagine that anyone would really care for me or want me around."

DeeDee has tears of her own. "Of course we're still friends. Why wouldn't we be?"

"Dr. Rowe says it's very important that I learn to see myself as worthwhile. It's easy for her to say. When you're crazy wild all the time, you don't feel you can do the things that other people do; you feel like you've given up your rights. Please, I'm sorry for this babbling, but I can't seem to stop."

"If it makes you feel better," she says.

"These are not tears of despair, DeeDee, these are tears of joy, caused by so much goodness."

"I know what you mean, Grace."

After we separate, Miss Braverman gives us a tissue packet; we begin wiping our eyes.

"I'm glad you came. At first I was embarrassed and tense, but now I'm glad."

Miss Braverman says, "It looks like we made the right decision, DeeDee."

"She means about deciding to come and visit," says DeeDee. "We talked it over for quite a while and asked your mother. I wanted you to see the science project, you worked so hard on it."

"Why don't we all sit down now?" says Miss Braverman. "Let's have some tea." She has taken a beige Thermos and three small cups and saucers from her large woven handbag. She sets everything on the coffee table in front of the couch. "We don't have cream or sugar, but the tea should still be warm."

I look at DeeDee and I start to giggle. "You told her."

DeeDee is also giggling. "You said it was a fantasy, but you never said it was a secret; you never said I couldn't tell anybody."

Miss Braverman is pouring.

I say, "Actually, it's against the rules to bring any food or drink from the outside."

"If you promise not to tell, I promise not to tell," says Miss Braverman. She smiles, and screws the cap back on the Thermos.

"It's too bad we don't have any munchies," says DeeDee.

But the words are scarcely out of her mouth, when I remember the cookie. I sit up straight as a post. "We do, though, we do! Please wait just a moment, I'll be right back."

I run up the stairs as fast as I can, and down the hall to my room. I rescue the cookie from beneath the pillow and run all the way

113

back. "Let's use the cookie," I say, fighting for breath. "It's so big, we can break it. It isn't perfect, but it's better than nothing. My appetite is improving anyway, and why should the cookie just sit there and disintegrate into crumbs?"

"I think this cookie will be just the thing," says Miss Braverman. She breaks it into half a dozen small chunks and spreads the chunks on a Kleenex.

We start nibbling the chunks and sipping our tea. "Would you like to hear about the science fair?" asks Miss Braverman.

"Yes, please," I say. "I'm still out of breath and I would like to hear about it."

"It's held on the last Saturday of October, at the University. We'll be taking one of the school vans. Besides you and DeeDee, there are three other students going. There's a ten-dollar entrance fee for each project, and we'll have to buy a couple of meals."

"It sounds wonderful," I say. "We will spend the day together and eat our meals together. It will be so much togetherness."

"I think you'll enjoy it," Miss Braverman says. "There are always so many fascinating exhibits."

"Up in my room I have thirty dollars, and Dr. Rowe says I'll be getting out of the hospital before too much longer."

"It sounds like we have a date, then."

DeeDee says she hopes the van is air-conditioned because the weather has been so hot.

"According to the paper, we've broken four heat records already this month," says Miss Braverman.

"It's more like July than October," says DeeDee. "And it's so dry. I wish we'd get a little rain. I have to water my little trees every night."

"It's unseasonably warm and dry," I say. "The earth is parched and cracking, and the grass is brown and brittle."

114

Miss Braverman is laughing. "Isn't this a fine thing; we come to visit Grace and the best we can do is talk about the weather."

"Oh no, Miss Braverman," I say. "It's perfect, really. The weather is a very appropriate topic. We are three women having tea together. Everything is so nice, I wish I could think of a better word, but it's just so nice. We have even eaten the cookie."

She smiles and says, "You do understand that we miss you."

"I believe it to be true. I'd like to tell you how nice everything is, but I'm afraid I'll start to cry again."

Seven

10/14

Dear Diary:

   Schizoaffective disorder (manic or depressive or mixed) *is applied to individuals who show features of both schizophrenia and affective disorder. In the DSM-III classification, this disorder is not listed as a formal category of schizophrenic disorder, but rather under "Psychotic disorders not elsewhere classified." This no doubt reflects the fact that schizoaffective disorder presents something of a taxonomic problem, and current controversy prevails over whether these persons should be considered basically schizophrenic or basically affectively disordered, or a group unto themselves. Probably most clinicians lean in the direction of the first choice, although the course of the disorder (rapid onset and rapid resolution) more nearly approximates that usually seen in the affective psychoses.*

I don't know why I have written these sentences in my diary. They aren't my own sentences, they come from a textbook; but Dr. Rowe said I could write whatever I wanted.

   The cover design for Marx and Ginsberg's book is a whirling blue and white sky. It is a detail of a painting by Van Gogh called *Ravine in the Peyroulets.* Is it possible that Van Gogh lived with the sky voice? Did his spinning sky send him warnings?

   My eyes scan the subheadings listed in the chapter called *The Schizophrenias:* Undifferentiated. Catatonic. Disorganized.

116

Hebephrenic. Reactive. Progressive. Residual. Schizoaffective. Schizotypal. Process. Schizophreniform.

Too much data loses its meaning. It is very appropriate to have a Van Gogh cover on a textbook about madness, but I close the book and put it back on the shelves. I'm quite sure Marx and Ginsberg have studied lots and lots of cases in some hospital somewhere, but my brain can't absorb any more data about crazy people.

I am calm but bored. Sometimes the evenings are so boring. I don't like watching television or shooting pool or playing Ping-Pong. Maybe I should take up woodworking. I would like to go home now; Dr. Rowe says I can probably go home in a few days, if everything goes well. If I do go home, the Surly People will be there and I'm afraid I will get scrambled again. It's discouraging to be suspended always in the same limbo.

I walk slowly down the north hall. All the doors on both sides are closed, but the green line leads me. At the shop door, the light is shining through the frosted glass. It's odd, at this time of night, for someone to be there. I stop and listen. There are creaking and cracking sounds, as if someone is prying boards apart.

I wonder if it is Mr. Sneed behind the door. My hand reaches out to touch the doorknob, but I quickly pull it back. Mr. Sneed is kind, but it could be someone else.

I have talked to Mr. Sneed about woodworking; I have told him of the times my father used to take me to the shop at the high school. Mr. Sneed teaches woodworking groups and spends a lot of time in the shop. He would enjoy talking to me, and I to him.

I reach out again and touch the doorknob. A knot is forming in my stomach; *what if it's not Mr. Sneed?* My hand turns the knob slowly until I hear it click. I push the door gently so that it eases open, about two feet.

It is Luke. I am standing and staring, and he is looking straight at me.

"What do you want?"

"I'm sorry; I thought it was Mr. Sneed."

"Yeah, well, what do you want?"

The knot is hard and my pulse is racing. "I meant no harm, really. I just thought you were Mr. Sneed." I stop talking as the words catch in my throat, and I hurry to moisten my mouth.

"Hey look, Red," he says. "If you wanta come in and shoot the shit, that's cool, but don't stand there holdin' the door open, huh?"

"Do you mean we should talk with each other?"

In the moment before he can answer, I relive the terror of the hallway at school, the Surly People with their painted swastikas and their hot breath and their groping fingers, and the cruel shadow of Mr. Stereo. The one called Luke is probably one of them; I should leave now.

"All I'm sayin' is, either come in or get out, but don't stand there holdin' the door open. I want it shut."

I don't know what it is that makes me hesitate. I should leave now. If I went inside the room I would be all alone with him, and that would put me at risk. I looked at the Surly People through the slits on my balcony and it terrified me, but I had to go on looking.

Something I don't understand is leading me. With the panic still locked inside me, I step across the threshold and inside the room. I close the door behind me.

Immediately, I sit down on a shop stool near the door and begin to take deep breaths. My father used to take me to the shop at the high school and sometimes I helped him build things. Luke is prying apart some dirty skids, the kind used by forklifts. He is using a small crowbar and his well-defined muscles are bulging. The rusty spiral nails are ripped out screeching.

118

I sit and watch. I feel conspicuous and uncomfortable, but for some reason my panic is subsiding.

After a few minutes, he takes a break and lights a Marlboro. He slouches against a workbench.

"What are you working on?" I ask timidly.

"I'm tearin' some of these skids apart to get the lumber. These two-bys are solid oak."

"Are you going to build something?"

"I was thinkin' of makin' a couple coffee tables. It would beat the hell out of makin' more of those horseshit ashtrays and candy dishes."

It reminds me of what my father would do; make something useful or beautiful out of something discarded. But it seems absurd, comparing Luke to my father.

"It sounds like a nice idea," I say. "But the skids. Where do they come from?"

"I got them from the parking lot."

"You mean you left the building?"

He takes a long drag and exhales some irregular smoke rings. "Well, they sure as hell weren't gonna walk in here all by themselves."

He is frightening and yet I chose to be alone with him. A sign on the door says, NO ADMITTANCE. STAFF ONLY. I ask, "Are you supposed to be here?"

"In a way," he says. He smiles, and his teeth are straight and regular. He has such a nice smile, and so much hygiene, but I have seen his anger and I suspect his brutality.

"Please," I say, "I don't understand."

"I was watchin' TV up in the lounge. I was bad-mouthin' *The Cosby Show,* and it got Sarbanes and a few others all unglued. Mrs. Higgins told me to go find somethin' to do. So here I am, with somethin' to do."

119

"But wasn't the door locked?"

"Of course. You've heard of the old credit card trick, haven't you?"

"Yes, but do you have a credit card?"

"No. I have a library card. It's made of plastic, like a credit card."

"If you have a library card, it must mean that you read books."

"Yeah, from time to time I do. Hey look, Red, is this gonna be 'Twenty Questions' or what?"

"I'm sorry, I meant no harm."

"Yeah, well, don't wet your pants. I've never kissed ass in my life, and I'm not gonna do it in this hospital."

My pulse has quickened again and there are tears stinging my eyes. I blink them back. "I'm sorry, really I am. I am only trying to make conversation to the best of my ability, but I'm not very good at it."

"Yeah, okay, like I'm sorry I got stiff with you. I'll get twenty questions when I go to court, I don't need it now."

"I forgot that you have to go to trial. Please forgive me. I only meant about the books that we may have something in common. I read books all the time. Dr. Rowe and my mother think I read too much because it is a solitary activity which I use as a means of withdrawal. When I'm flat out I don't read at all, I lose interest in just about everything."

"I wouldn't know about that," says Luke. "Most of this shit about psychopaths and stuff goes right over my head. Most of what I read is stuff out of the sixties. That was a time when people took no shit. They stood up to just about every bullshitter there was, and told them to kiss ass."

"My father was active in the Vietnam protest movement," I say. "He was even in the march on Washington in 'sixty-nine."

"Your old man sounds like a cool dude."

"He's dead now. He was very dear to me, we were like best friends. My Uncle Larry died in Vietnam. His name is inscribed on the Vietnam monument in Washington, D.C. Sometime I would like to go there and run my fingers over his chiseled name; it would be comforting because it would prove he wasn't overlooked."

"That's a bummer about your old man and your uncle, Red; some of your phraseology is pretty weird though."

"My father and I used to go for walks at Allerton. We went several times a week in nice weather. Our house was on the Allerton estate, near the park."

"I know the place you're talkin' about," he says. He is grinding out his cigarette butt on the floor. "It's downstate; I've been there."

"You've been to Allerton Park?" This information makes me uneasy.

"A couple of times for drug seminars. We got this new supervisor at Clark House last year named Spellmyer. About the first thing he did was load us all up and take us there for drug seminars."

"They use the mansion for conferences and seminars," I say. "But are you a drug user?"

He waves his hand. "Hell no. I've smoked a little pot from time to time, that's about it. You tell that to a bullshitter, though, and he figures you're a junkie or a dealer. Or both."

It still stuns me that he's been to Allerton. "Did you like the park?" I ask him.

He shrugs and says, "It was okay. There wasn't much action there. You got to remember, we were listenin' to bullshitters day and night. There was this huge statue of a naked guy with his arms out; we climbed up and put a rubber on his pecker." He laughs harshly at the memory.

He's talking about the Sunsinger. "A rubber?"

"Yeah, you know; a condom." He laughs hard again.

He's talking about the Sunsinger. The Sunsinger greets the

121

morning sun every day; he greets the eye. You must remember what Dr. Rowe says: the eye is a delusion just as surely as the voice is. But Luke defiled the statue; he is Surly, why have I chosen to be here with him?

He's not aware that I am embarrassed or offended. He says, "Anyway, gettin' back to the subject, I figure I was born into the wrong time in history. I've got a few paperbacks back in my room at home — *Slaughterhouse Five* and one called *Soul on Ice,* and a real good book on the Hell's Angels." He takes off his headband, wipes some sweat from his forehead onto the back of his wrist, and then puts the headband back on.

Without a warning, he wants to change the subject. He asks me what I'm in for.

"I thought I already told you," I say quickly. "I'm crazy wild and I don't fit in."

"Yeah, but there has to *be* something. With me, it was pullin' Johnny's plug; that's what I'm in for."

"I was molested and it was too traumatic. It precipitated my current psychotic state. Once I tried suicide but it didn't work. They put me in for the longest time and gave me shock treatments." I need to be very careful — the sky could return at any moment if I reveal too much. He defiled the statue.

"You tried to snuff? You shouldn't do a thing like that."

"Please, I was so desperate, I don't think I could explain it. Besides, didn't we agree that there are worse things than death?"

"Yeah, that's true, but not for a person like you, with a good mind. I have a lot of respect for a good mind."

Is he trying to encourage me? What kind of conversation this is I know not. "I don't mean to be quarrelsome, but I think it would be better to be stupid and in control."

"When you tried to snuff, how did you do it?"

122

"I cut my wrists in the bathtub. Please, there is static; I don't want to talk about it anymore."

He shrugs and says, "That's cool. It's up to you." He begins putting lumber away in the lower cabinets.

I say, "I would rather talk about your foster homes."

He shrugs again. "What's to say?"

"Please, I would never be impertinent. I've always been so close to my mother and father, I can't imagine what it would be like to grow up without a family. Did you ever know your parents at all?"

"No. And I only lived in a foster home once. Mostly, it was group homes. Right now I'm livin' at Clark House; they moved me there from Haig House."

"Why did they move you?"

"I got expelled from East High for gettin' in too many fights. That's why they put me in Clark House. Clark House is for bad asses. I guess somebody thinks I'm a bad ass."

He fights. He is brutal. But the static has diminished and I feel I will not get scrambled. I would like to ask him about the fighting, but I am afraid.

He says, "When I was goin' to East High, these guys were squeezin' me. They wanted me to join this gang called the Silkworms. I told 'em to shove it; I never join gangs. If you're a member of a gang, it means you don't go your own way. They couldn't handle it, so they put me on their list."

"It seems so unfair. All you wanted was to be left alone. If you don't have to go to prison will they let you return to Clark House?"

"Who knows? Some bullshitter will decide that. Eight months from now I'll be eighteen; I'll have the system off my back and I'll go my own way." He has finished putting the lumber away. He closes the cabinet doors and stands up.

123

"You are vulnerable," I say suddenly, without thinking. "A remarkable thought has occurred to me."

"What's that supposed to mean?"

"The system makes you vulnerable because it holds you in its grip. I am vulnerable because everything threatens and frightens me, but I have my mother. No one can put my mother and me apart."

He says, "If you're vulnerable, that means you're somebody's victim. Somebody has a hold over you. Take my word, I am nobody's victim."

"Please don't feel insulted. It was just a thought which occurred to me."

"Okay, so here's the thought that occurs to me: I don't want your pity or anybody's pity. When it comes to pity, I piss on it. A bullshitter can put me in jail, but he can't get inside my head. He can't control my thoughts. Bullshitters are never happy if they can't control your mind."

He has minor static again. "I meant no harm, really."

"That's another thing. You can't go around comin' unglued every time a person says something. Let's get the hell out of here. You get the lights while I fix this lock."

*

It is only two days later that he sits by me at lunch in the cafeteria. There are many available chairs, but he chooses the one next to mine. His presence makes me tense, but I am not frightened.

There is meat loaf with gravy on my tray; I couldn't warn the staff in time to leave it off. I pick at my gravyless mashed potatoes and my applesauce. Luke shovels his food in aggressively.

For a few minutes we don't speak, and then I say, "I would like to tell you something, if you don't mind."

"It's a free country."

124

"Miss Ivey is gone. They have moved her to another facility. It was only a matter of time."

He talks with his mouth full: "You mean the old chick that watches TV all the time?"

"Yes."

He shrugs, then I tell him, "They sent her to another institution. Mrs. Grant told me how the procedure works. If you're catatonic, and they think you're not going to get any better, they send you to a long-term facility; this hospital is not a long-term facility."

His mouth is still full, but he speaks anyway: "That's how it was gonna be for Johnny, except he still had his mind. Miss Ivey was more or less brain-dead, so she won't know the difference. What's the big deal anyway, was she a friend of yours or something?"

"Not exactly. It's just the loss of hope. It's one of my greatest fears. I'm afraid that some day I will be just like her, and they will have to find a long-term facility for me." I don't know why I am telling him about my fears; if he is laying the trap which the sky has predicted, I am walking into it.

"I doubt if that'll happen," he says.

"I'm sure you're trying to offer encouragement, but don't forget I've done research on the pathological mind. It's the only prognosis for my life which makes sense."

He shrugs again. I decide it will be less threatening if he talks about himself. "Your friend John sounds like a very curious person. How did the two of you become friends?"

"I was workin' at the dodo house, and he made deliveries for this provision company. After we unloaded his truck, the two of us would sit around and shoot the shit."

"Excuse me, but do retarded people have a house of their own?"

"Yeah. The same agency runs it that runs Clark House. If you live at Clark House, and you keep your nose clean, they'll give you a little work at the dodo house. You can earn a few bucks that way.

125

The truth is, I always liked the dodos; they were just who they were and they never gave any shit. Anyway, John was just out of the navy. They kicked him out on a section eight."

"What is a section eight?"

"A medical discharge. Unfit for military service. He went AWOL for a few days but caught pneumonia. The MPs brought him back. He kept getting shrink interviews and telling officers to get bent. It was probably less hassle to just give him the section eight and get rid of him. I could tell he was a guy who would do his own thing and take no grief from anybody."

I nibble at my green beans. His friend John scares me but I don't want to tell him that. He goes on, "I never talk about this stuff. My social worker wants to know all this shit, but she's just another bullshitter so I usually tell her zilch. It must be that I like you."

"It would be very odd for you to like me," I say quickly. "We are so different. My friend DeeDee likes me and I think Dr. Rowe does too. Apparently I have redeeming qualities, but they're not usually at the surface."

"You sure have a way with words, Red. Anyway, to get on with it, John told me he was blowin' off the delivery job and gettin' ready to go on the road, takin' his Harley; he asked me if I wanted to go with him. He didn't have to ask me twice, I was already on pro at Clark House, and if it meant gettin' free and clear of social workers and other bullshitters, I was ready. What John had in mind was followin' the crops. Migrant work, in other words."

"But I don't understand how a person can find migrant work. Can you just drop everything and go?"

"This was back in June. There's guys that know the system of followin' the crops, like this one guy we got to know named Ruiz. The first job we got was pickin' strawberries on a couple farms close to Benton Harbor, Michigan. The work was hard and you couldn't make much money because you got paid by the quart. For sleeping,

126

we had these sort of dormitories. I didn't care too much about the money, I was just glad to be on my own."

It does feel safer when he talks about himself. I say to him, "I can't imagine the courage it would take to go out on the road like that and fend for yourself, on your own resources."

"You could imagine it if you'd spent your life in places like Clark House. A girl on the road, though, that might be somethin' else, I'm not sure. Anyway, the strawberries were finished in a couple weeks, then we went up and picked blueberries for a while close to a place called Muskegon."

His bold story fascinates me. He pauses to finish his milk, then goes on. "We went for some R and R one weekend in Benton Harbor. We ended up spendin' a few nights at a stripper's house named Tina. I had my own bedroom and John was sleepin' with Tina. In the daytime he was drinking wine most of the time and doin' grass with Tina."

He is telling me his adventures with some whore. I've never had a talk like this in my life.

"Anyway, bein' at Tina's house was pretty boring. For me, that is. John wasn't bored at all. I finally told him I thought we ought to get back on the road and make some cash. He said he was mellowed out with Tina, why didn't I just go on ahead and he would catch up with me later on. I was a little funked, but what could I say? It was his business and besides, there's no guarantees on the road."

He wants to get close. The voice is warning me. *But he doesn't really like you. Can't you see how clever it is?*

"I went out and picked some more blueberries and then some cherries for a few days. Then I went about a week with no work. It was harder to find work because I had to hitch; John had the bike. I got bummed out. It just wasn't the same without him and I never did run into Ruiz again. I said the hell with it and hitched my way

127

back home. The shit hit the fan at Clark House. I went from pro to strict pro."

"I'm so sorry, it seems so sad. You had high expectations. When did you find him in the hospital?"

"That was later." He looks at my plate. "You must not be hungry."

"My appetite is usually poor. Today is no exception."

"You haven't even touched your meat loaf."

"Please, I'm vegetarian. I couldn't eat it even if I wanted to. Would you like to have it?"

"You sure?"

"Oh yes, I'm quite sure. I'd like you to have it."

"What the hell, if it's just goin' in the garbage." He takes my tray and scrapes the meat loaf onto his own. He begins devouring it.

Then he touches my arm, without speaking. I look quickly into his eyes and he nods his head in the direction of the far end of the table. In a very low voice which is hardly more than a whisper, he says: "That's my roommate. That's the dodo I was talkin' about."

I turn my head and look. A thin boy with black hair, who looks about eighteen, is sitting across the table from Mrs. Youngblood and Miss Sloan, another therapist.

I turn back to Luke and whisper: "What's his name?"

"His name is Chris; they're goofin' on him. Check it out."

I look again. Mrs. Youngblood is telling Chris that he needs to eat slowly and take little bites. Chris takes a bite of meat loaf, then Mrs. Youngblood pulls his tray away from him. She tells him, "You chew that bite properly and swallow it, and then you may have your tray again." She smiles at Miss Sloan.

He takes another bite and she pulls the tray away again. With no warning, Chris snaps his head forward violently three or four times and turns red in the face. Mrs. Youngblood smiles and arches her

128

eyebrows. She says to Miss Sloan, "We don't like this one little bit, do we?"

They are taunting him. It's hard for me to believe what I'm seeing.

They repeat the procedure, only this time Chris whips his head more violently and barks like a dog. Mrs. Youngblood and Miss Sloan giggle at each other and Mrs. Youngblood repeats her words: "No sir, we don't like this one little bit."

Why are they doing this? I feel so sorry for him, it's cruel and unfair. I see for the briefest moment in my mind's eye the cruelty of the Surly People when they taunted me with firecrackers and relished my suffering.

I turn back to Luke, but his eyes have gone hard and glittery like gemstones.

"There must be something we can do," I say. "It's not right for them to treat him this way. But there's nothing we can do."

"Keep your voice down," he says, without looking at me. His brittle eyes are locked on the far end of the table. I know immediately that something terrible is about to happen; my breathing tightens and my scalp begins to prickle.

I look once more, and it is so pathetic. Chris is head-whipping and barking like a dog. The two women are giggling like adolescents.

Suddenly, with the back of his hand, Luke knocks his tray to the floor, where it lands with a loud clatter. Then with his other hand, he knocks my tray to the floor.

He stands up, facing Mrs. Youngblood. He says to her, "You prime bullshitter, leave him the hell alone."

The whole cafeteria has gone silent. Mrs. Youngblood has gone white with fear — the panicky fear of being discovered.

Mrs. Youngblood orders Luke to sit down, and she tells Miss Sloan to call security.

Luke grabs the table and flips it over; its edge smashes on the floor so hard it seems to shake the building. Chris has stopped barking and started to cry. Everything is charged with static and I am shaking like a leaf; I wonder how much more of this I will see before I get scrambled.

Mr. Sneed comes with another security man. The two of them grab Luke by the arms but he flings them away. He is violent and dangerous beyond comprehension, yet I have let him into my life. Invited him, practically.

There are bodies flying and dishes breaking. There are people screaming and sobbing. Flashbulbs are exploding in my brain and I wonder if I'm about to black out. Then the mist comes.

Eight

THIS IS THE first time in a week that I have been with Dr. Rowe. I wish I could see her more often, it is comforting to have her insight. But there are so many other people who need help.

I have been flat out for three days. My appearance is particularly neglected and repulsive, but who cares? Mother was here last night to bring me more homework and give me one of her pep talks. It seemed so desperate, it caused me to weep bitterly. My grades will be poor.

Dr. Rowe wants to hear about my mother's visit.

"I told her I don't want to be in the hospital anymore. I asked her to take me home."

"Is that what you want?"

I shrug and say, "I don't know. Sometimes it is."

"What about now? Is it what you want now?"

"I don't know. You don't think I should go home, do you?"

"No," says Dr. Rowe. "I don't think you're ready. What did your mother say?"

"She said I should ask for a pass."

"Would you like a pass, Grace? Would you like to go home for the weekend?"

"I think I would. I think I would like a pass."

"All right then. You're flat out, aren't you, Grace? Don't be lazy. We need to make good use of our time together."

You can't get anything past her, but what does she really know? Her life is sound. I'm sure she has martinis at six with her husband

and puts the crazy people out of her mind. Well, why shouldn't she? My mother is so good, and I am such a sorrow to her. I am an embarrassing open sore that won't close. If I died, my mother's life would be purified. If I died, the world would not miss a beat.

"Dr. Rowe, I had the train dream again."

"Was it the same?"

"It's always the same."

She waits a few moments. Then she says, "Tell me about it. Don't hide from me."

That's what she always says, but I know she means well. I force myself to speak: "The train is fast and loud; it terrifies me. It explodes into my head. It causes my whole room to vibrate, and I sit on my bed with the shakes. Then the mist comes."

She waits a few moments then says, "Is there any more?"

"Sometimes, when the train comes, I wet the bed. It is quite humiliating."

"Grace, let me see the train. Draw me a picture."

"It is a locomotive. It roars and hisses steam."

She answers, "A locomotive suggests power, and force, and energy. The train may simply represent your unconscious, trying to find its way into consciousness."

"I'm afraid I wouldn't know much about power or force."

"You do though. Those qualities are a part of you, just as they are a part of me or any person. The unconscious part of you is not just ugly and dangerous, it is also resourceful and creative."

"But the train is so scary."

"It is indeed, but so is your unconscious. It wants to become part of you, but you repress it and suppress it. You fear it and resist it so completely that you have divided yourself."

Her voice is starting to crackle. When she speaks to me like this I feel like I'm being scolded. I blink back the tears which are forming and sit up straight. I fold my legs into the lotus position.

132

Dr. Rowe continues, "Grace, deep down inside, in your unconscious, you have decided that life is a battlefield. A place of enemies and adversaries. Your father went like a hero to do battle, but you can't."

I say, "My father went to do battle while Mother stayed at home to darn socks."

"Yes. Exactly. Participating in life is like going to war. Life is treachery and life is danger."

She has such insight but her static makes things confusing. "I'll tell you one thing for sure," I say. "I don't know much about trains, I don't think I've ever ridden on a train in my life."

She says, "Grace, if the train is frightening, try and think of it this way: you won't allow your unconscious to reveal itself in a conventional way, or a natural way, so it forces itself through in an unnatural and uncomfortable way. One thing's for sure: your unconscious won't simply go away, as much as you might want it to."

"You're saying I'm pretty sick."

She lights one of her cigarettes. "I'm trying to say that the things which upset you are the consequences of the way you have divided yourself. When you learn to receive and accept some of the unconscious elements of yourself, you will begin to get better."

I understand the logic of the point she is making, but I want to change the subject. I tell her so.

"What would you like to tell me?" she asks.

"I need to tell you about Luke Wolfe."

"Okay, what do you want to say about him?"

I lick my lips. "When he lost his temper in the cafeteria, he was provoked. I saw the whole thing. I was wondering if you could please release him from lockup."

"I can't do that, Grace."

"But he really was provoked."

"How was he provoked?"

133

"Mrs. Youngblood and Miss Sloan were taunting his roommate, the one called Chris. They were manipulating him. It was cruel."

"How were they manipulating him?"

"They were teasing him with his food to get him to react, then they were laughing at him. They have no right. I know how unlikely it sounds, but I am telling the truth."

Dr. Rowe is making notes. She says to me, "I thought you said Luke frightened you. I thought you wanted to be as far away from him as possible."

"He has much violence and an explosive temper, but I think he has redeeming qualities; I think he is not evil. He never knew his parents. Please, Dr. Rowe, I would never tell you how to do your job, but he was provoked."

"Don't apologize; I'm encouraged to see you sticking up for him. But I can't release him from lockup. His loss of control proves that he is a potential danger to other patients. I went out on a limb for him once, but I have to consider the safety of all the patients on this unit. Not to mention the staff."

"But Dr. Rowe, please believe me."

"It's not that I don't believe you, Grace. I will look into what you are telling me. But even if he was provoked, the provocation was not equal to his reaction. Luke's life is not going to work until he learns something about appropriate ways of dealing with problems."

I'm not sure she truly believes me, but I have already argued far beyond my normal limits. My throat is tight but I say, "Then may I please visit him?"

"You want to visit him?"

"Please, I'd like to visit him on lockup. I feel sorry for him."

She is putting out her cigarette. For several moments, she looks at me without speaking. She finally says, "You were terrified of him. What has happened to the fear?"

My eyes are suddenly filled with tears. I'm going to start crying, but I don't know why. I never know why. "I'm still scared of him. But he is a human being and I feel sorry for him."

"Of course he's a human being."

Now the tears are running down my face. "I'm sorry for crying so much."

"You don't need to apologize. Tears are fine."

"But they don't feel fine, why are they fine?"

"Because emotions at the surface are better than buried emotions. Especially in your case."

"Dr. Rowe, I want to understand things, but I can't." I wipe my face but the tears keep coming. "I don't know if the medicine makes me better or not. I don't know if I would be the same without the medicine or worse."

Dr. Rowe doesn't speak.

"Everything gets so electrical and there's so much data. I don't know if my problems are biological or psychological."

"Or both?"

"Or both."

"Or neither?" I look at her smile. Then she says, "We were talking about Luke. You want to visit him."

I blow my nose and tell her, "I think I would like to visit him. Would it be okay?"

"I think it would be just fine. It would probably be beneficial to him if he did have a visitor."

"Thank you."

"You'll have to wait until tomorrow. I know that he's tied up today with lawyers and social workers."

"Thank you."

*

At six A.M. there is only the hint of gray lifting the darkness. I awake refreshed from a restful night's sleep and slip into my robe. I

135

follow the blue line, past the nurses' station, through the lounge, down the north hallway, and into the cafeteria.

"Please Mrs. Bonner, if you don't mind, I'd like a cup of tea."

There are staff members sitting at some of the tables, drinking coffee, but I do not listen to their conversations; I wait for my tea.

When the hot water comes, it is in a Styrofoam cup. Dipping my teabag as I go, I walk back to the lounge, but since it is now the latter part of October, the windows by the blue couch are closed. I go out through the double doors that lead to the parking lot, where I sit on the concrete ledge which borders some evergreen shrubs. I continue dipping my tea. There is not enough light to see the highway, but I can hear tires whining in the distance. Tomorrow is Saturday and I will go home with my mother for the weekend; I know this is so because Dr. Rowe has written me a pass.

The first streaks of pale pink are layered along the eastern sky. A cool breeze is firm from the northwest. The breeze carries the smell of fresh manure from the university farm, and the lowing of the cattle. They are lined up for milking, the way that cows have done for thousands of years. They are the roots of the whole world, rooted deep and firm.

Cooooo ooooo ooooo
Oooooo ooooo ooooo

I look for the dove and find her perched on the power line overhead. Her graceful tail-feathers are flared like a swallow's tail. The dove brings peace and harmony while I sip my tea slowly.

Cooooo ooooo ooooo
Ooooo ooooo ooooo

The cool breeze turns chilly; I pull my robe up tight around my neck. I sip the tea as best I can, but my teeth have started to chatter. The light is stronger now, and I can see the interstate.

136

"Grace, how long have you been out here?"

It is Mrs. Higgins. Her abrupt voice startles me.

"Grace, you'll catch your death of cold out here. Please come inside."

"I don't think it's been long. I'm never sure of the time."

"You haven't had your medication yet."

"It's so quiet and peaceful here. I'm listening to the dove."

"You heard me, Grace. Come inside please."

We go inside and she gives me my medicine.

"Dr. Rowe has interpreted the train dream for me."

"That's good, Grace, but you are shivering and your teeth are chattering. How does a nice hot bath sound?"

"That would be very nice, Mrs. Higgins; it might have an element of purification."

"I want you to have some breakfast first."

I pick at breakfast without appetite or enthusiasm. I drink my orange juice.

Mrs. Higgins takes me to the tub room so I can soak in bubble-bath. She sits in a chair next to the tub. I don't mind that she looks at me while I'm naked; the process of purification has many parts.

"I understand you're visiting Luke this morning."

"Yes, that's true. I forgot."

"I think you'll look lovely when we're finished here."

"Mrs. Higgins, it's only one patient visiting another. Did I mention that Dr. Rowe has interpreted my train dream?"

"Yes, you did mention it, and I said I was happy to hear it." She hands me a white plastic Bic razor, which I use for shaving my legs, until the skin is slick and clean. It takes longer to shave my armpits, where the hair is dense.

"Mrs. Higgins, it was in a bathtub like this that I cut my wrists."

"I know."

137

"The water was crimson billows, like swift-moving storm clouds."

"Does it serve any purpose for us to talk about it?"

"No, you're quite right about that."

"Here's a bottle of conditioner. Would you like to try it?"

She's trying to make me over. I use shampoo and then conditioner until my hair is squeaky clean. I stand in front of the mirror and dry off with a fluffy white towel. After I use the towel to squeeze the heaviest moisture from my hair, Mrs. Higgins plugs in a red Clairol blow drier.

My body is dry. I step into a pair of clean white underpants.

"Do you have a clean bra?" Mrs. Higgins wants to know.

"I don't have any bra at all, Mrs. Higgins. I never wear one."

She makes no comment, but hands me the blow drier. It whines out its heat as I go, lifting my hair. When my hair is dry and full, I give it several strokes with the hairbrush to give it shape. It's hard to see properly because the mirror is steamed.

She gives me baby powder, which I rub on my neck and shoulders and underarms. Then she shapes my broken fingernails with a nail file, and applies some clear gloss nail polish.

I spread my fingers and admire my glistening, oval fingernails. I now have the hands of a lady and my armpits are slick and fragrant.

"You have made me a new woman," I say to Mrs. Higgins.

"You look lovely, Grace. Doesn't it make you feel better?"

"It's very nice, Mrs. Higgins, but on the inside I'm still the same person."

"How would you like to try a little make-up?"

"What kind of make-up? I know nothing of make-up."

"Nothing heavy, maybe just a little mascara."

She darkens my eyelashes with mascara, then applies a touch of blush to my cheeks and a tiny bit of orange lip gloss.

"You look lovely," she declares. "Let me look at you."

"Thank you very much, Mrs. Higgins. I feel better too, but I don't have any clothes on. I need to get dressed now."

I go back to my room so I can finish dressing. I am going to visit Luke on lockup but I will not be afraid. I look in the mirror; the face in the mirror has make-up and mascara, but it is still my face.

To get to the lockup wing, you have to follow the yellow line. It leads down long corridors to the right and to the left and continues on beyond the end of the blue line. But what if the lines ran out? What if they disappeared? I will not be afraid; I will visit Luke and we will find a way to make conversation.

And then suddenly, without a warning, the voice comes:

Only three short weeks ago, he filled you with fear. You must not go to him. He is one of them.

The voice wants in but I must not honor it.

He stands with the forces of darkness. He has seduced you.

I press my hands over my ears and keep walking. There is the yellow line ahead of me. He has redeeming qualities. He never knew his parents.

He is a psychopath. He murdered his friend and he devastated the cafeteria. Can you blind yourself to every piece of evidence?

He was provoked; I was there.

He has seduced you. He is one of them. If evil always appeared evil, it would not be insidious.

I say out loud, "I don't have to listen to you. You are not real, and you are not my father. You are a delusion."

I will not be afraid; I will visit Luke and we will know what to say to each other.

The double doors at the entrance to the lockup unit are locked; they have very small windows with wire mesh. A nurse I have never seen before sits in a glass cubicle; she slides a panel and asks me what I want.

I tell her I would like to visit Luke, and she says, "You need a pass to visit a patient on this unit. Whose patient are you?"

"Dr. Rowe's patient. She gave me permission to visit him."

"You need to get a pass from Dr. Rowe. If she wants you to talk to Luke, she'll write you one."

"Please, could you call her? I only want to talk to him for a few minutes, then I'll leave."

"I'm trying to tell you there's a procedure for this. You need a written pass."

She has static now. "But could you please just call her? I didn't know about the written pass."

The nurse picks up the phone with an annoyed look on her face. I hope I'm not becoming a pushy person; it isn't polite to be pushy. She speaks on the phone and then she tells me, "You may speak to Luke, but not longer than thirty minutes. In the future though, you'll need a written pass from Dr. Rowe if you want to speak to him. Do you understand?" She is getting a ring of keys from her pocket.

"Yes, I do understand," I say. "Thank you very much."

I talk to Luke in a small lounge area while the security guard leans on the counter at the nurses' station. He has his eye on us.

I ask Luke how he is doing and he shrugs. His hair is damp. He is wearing his blue kerchief headband and a white tee shirt with a logo that says *Crane Cams*. I don't know what it means, but it can't be important at this moment.

"You look real good," he says to me.

I am embarrassed. "Thank you very much, I'm not accustomed to hearing such things."

"You've done something with your hair. It looks real good."

"It's nice of you to say so," I say. "I am slick and fragrant, but the credit actually belongs to Mrs. Higgins."

Luke takes a Marlboro from the pack which is folded in his

140

sleeve. He lights up and says, "Bein' locked up in here, and the way you look, it's enough to give me a hard-on."

I can feel myself flushing madly and my pulse is starting to race. "Please, I wouldn't know about that. I don't understand; does this mean you have desire for me?"

"I've thought once or twice about gettin' in your pants, but that's only natural, am I right?" He is smiling his charming smile with all his teeth.

I need to breathe; I've never been spoken to like this before. "Can you say that to another person?"

"If you're gonna ask, you gotta let me answer."

When I am with him I feel like he is peeling me. The deep breathing will help me. The ones at school carried the mark of evil, but Luke is not one of them. "No one ever touched me before," I tell him. "No one ever kissed me either. DeeDee told me once about French kissing and it sounded repulsive. Dr. Rowe told me the Surly People who molested me were more interested in cruelty than in sex. She also showed me my father wasn't perfect and there's no such thing as Surly People, not in any organized sense. People are neither perfect nor perfectly evil."

He reaches over and touches the back of my hand. "I forgot all about the scumbags that tried to gang you, Red. I'm sorry for what I said."

There are tears blurring my eyes but the breathing helps me; I think I'll be okay. "I get confused about things; I shouldn't make such a big deal out of nothing."

"It was just a smartass remark," he says. "I apologize."

"It's okay. I'm not going to get scrambled, if that's what you mean. It would probably be a good idea if we changed the subject."

"That's cool." He shakes his loose hair and adjusts his headband. "If you want the truth," he says, "I think I owe you another apology."

141

"What for?"

"We were talkin' that one night about the place where you grew up."

"Allerton Park."

"Yeah. Allerton Park. It's a real nice place. I told you about puttin' a rubber on that statue; I didn't mean to hurt your feelings."

"You were only telling a story. I think my feelings get hurt too easily."

"Yeah, well anyway, I didn't mean to be disrespectful. I'm sorry. When we were down there, I remember layin' out under the stars on the shore of this pond. It was real, real peaceful there."

"That's the pond in front of the mansion," I say. "My father and I used to pick wildflowers in that area all the time." I now have my composure back, thanks to the deep breathing.

"It was pretty much a pure nature trip. It was real different from anything in my experience. That was in the summer though; what goes on down there this time of year?"

"Not much," I say. "After October fifteenth, the whole park is deserted, except on holidays. I always loved Allerton in late October and early November, when the trees had such glorious colors and I felt like I had the whole place to myself."

He is gazing off and blowing smoke at the ceiling. I decide to change the subject. "I'm so sorry you got put here. I told Dr. Rowe that you were provoked, but I'm not sure she believed me."

Luke looks at me for several seconds. "You stuck up for me?"

"I tried, but I'm not very good at it. I'm not exactly an assertive person. What good is my word against Mrs. Youngblood's?"

"Yeah, that's true. The bullshitters always seem to have the upper hand. That's how they control the system." He bends forward to put out his cigarette. Then he leans back in his chair and locks his hands behind his head. His legs are crossed at the ankles.

"I had about four bullshitters come and visit me yesterday," he says. "The main one was my caseworker. What it comes down to is, they're going to try me as an adult. I could be lookin' at a heavy-duty sentence."

"But why?"

"You tell me. It's not like I didn't cooperate. I told 'em I pulled Johnny's plug and I told 'em why. I even told 'em how."

"You told your caseworker the whole story?"

"Most of it. I gave her the highlights, you might say. I've never told anybody all the details about the actual part at the hospital. I'll tell you though, if you still want to hear it."

"Please tell me." I don't know whether to feel honored or afraid, but I know I want him to feel free to tell me.

He lights another cigarette. "This was a couple months after the migrant work adventure I told you about. It was around Labor Day, and I didn't actually know John was in the hospital until I got a letter from him. The person who actually wrote the letter was a hospital volunteer. I figured if he couldn't even write his own letter, he was probably in bad shape."

"But if your friend couldn't even talk or move, how did the hospital volunteer know to write the letter?"

"I think they found my address in Johnny's things."

"He knew you'd be back at your house?"

"No, hell no; after we split up, even I didn't know where I was headed. I think they just wrote the letter and hoped I'd get it. Anyhow, the hospital was clear over in the Quad Cities; I had to hitch. When I got there he was in intensive care. He was just skin and bones, I couldn't hardly even recognize him. His skin was gray. It was enough to make you bawl or piss your pants, just lookin' at him. I had a talk with this little old lady named Mrs. Askew. She was a hospital volunteer, in fact she was the one who wrote the letter. She told me it was almost a month since they brought John in. She said he was completely paralyzed from

143

damage to the spinal cord in a wipeout on the bike. I thought about how he liked to ride stoned, but I didn't mention that. She told me he wasn't goin' to get any better; they couldn't fix his spine. He couldn't eat or talk. They had to feed him through a tube. He even had to have his diapers changed by the nurses."

I am concentrating on what he is saying. I am trying to understand, so I don't say anything. I will see my mother tomorrow.

He goes on. "I had a long conversation with John in his room, which meant I was doin' the talkin'. All he could do was blink, once for yes and twice for no. To make a long story short, he wanted me to pull his plug. He wanted to snuff. That's the reason he wrote me the letter. When I left his room, I didn't say I would and I didn't say I wouldn't. I could understand his point of view, he'd been layin' there like a vegetable for almost a month, what did he have to look forward to in life, but snuffin' a guy is not the kind of thing you take lightly, you know what I mean? I had to think it over."

"If you were a true psychopath, you couldn't have as much conscience as you do."

"Thanks, Red. Anyhow, I went back to the hospital the next morning and had another talk with Mrs. Askew. My mind wasn't made up yet. I'm not usually into indecision; I knew I had to shit or get off the pot. Mrs. Askew was cuttin' up Styrofoam egg cartons for little kids in the hospital to do art projects. I was sincerely impressed; givin' her time to help hospital patients, gettin' no pay and probably no credit. In my opinion, people like her are worth a thousand bullshitters like Pendleton, he's the guy who runs Clark House, who spend their time in their BMWs or their fatass offices, gettin' their picture taken for the newspapers and makin' the decisions that run other peoples' lives.

"That's more or less off the subject. I just happen to remember it. I don't know how you get me to talk like this, Red. What Mrs.

Askew told me was, John didn't have any relatives to take care of him, so they were gonna send him to a state hospital for permanent placement. I said who made this decision, and she told me a hospital review board made up of doctors and social service people. As soon as she told me this, I got real steady inside and the decision was easy. John lived his whole life by his own code, free and clear of the system, and now the bullshitters were gonna put him in their vegetable garden for the rest of his life. It was either his way or their way, dependin' on what I decided to do. Lookin' at it that way, it was a simple choice."

"But I don't understand how you could do it. It must have taken skill and cleverness."

He shrugs. "It wasn't that hard. I think there was less nurses because it was a holiday weekend. Anyway, I went back about suppertime when everybody was busy servin' meals. I snuck into John's room without anybody seein' me. He was asleep, which was real important; I didn't want him to watch me do it."

"But weren't you scared?"

"A little, but not bad once my mind was made up. There was this big console close to his bed which was part of his respirator equipment. The respirator was the only thing keepin' him alive. When I took the panel off the back of the console, I found two or three electrical circuits. I didn't have time to study how the alarm was wired, so I just cut each one."

"Was he dead then?"

He shakes his head, "No. That was just to kill the alarm. The respirator was plugged into the wall down by the foot of the bed. Before I actually pulled the plug, I looked at him for a few seconds. He was skin and bones, but he was asleep and peaceful. I was real happy knowin' he was gonna go in his sleep. I just pulled the plug and left the room real quick without lookin' back. If he was gonna choke, I didn't want to be around to hear it."

145

He leans forward to put out the cigarette. "That's the story, Red. That's the whole thing. What do you think?"

It is so overwhelming because he is describing the actual death of a real person. "It's not for me to judge other people," I say quickly. "I have more than I can handle, just trying to deal with my own problems."

"Yeah, but what do you *think?*"

"You only meant it for his own good. You meant well."

"Tell it to the bullshitters." The faraway look is back in his eyes and it frightens me. "Sometimes I feel like my whole life is just gettin' the shaft, one way or another."

"Please don't say that."

"You said to me once I was vulnerable. Maybe you were right. I never shoulda been put in Clark House in the first place."

I wonder if I'm supposed to say something or ask a question, but I'm afraid; I have a lump in my stomach because I'm afraid he's leading up to something.

I tell him not to give up hope. I tell him maybe the court will be lenient; maybe the court will understand he meant well.

Luke shakes his head no and lowers his voice. "I need a favor, Red. I need a favor from you."

I am suddenly taking deep breaths. I have to stay in control, no matter what he asks.

His dark eyes have locked onto me. "I need to get out of here. I need to escape."

"But wouldn't that be unwise?" I ask. "Wouldn't that just make things worse?"

"Things can't get any worse. All I need is to get the hell out of here. I can make it on my own if I can get free."

"You mean I would help you escape." I hardly have the breath to say it.

"That's about the size of it."

I have a tight grip on the edge of my chair. "But this is the lockup wing, could you escape from here?"

"Yeah, I think so, but you'd have to give me a little help."

"How? What would I have to do?"

"All I'd need from you is a little distraction." He is speaking in a low voice, but trying to look natural.

"A distraction?"

"That's all. Just a little somethin' to keep old Four Eyes over there occupied for a minute or two."

I have to look away from his eyes. It's hard for me to concentrate on what he is saying, there's such a riot of feelings in my stomach. If there's something you want, you reach out and take it. How like the Surly People he seems at this moment.

He continues, "It's not gonna be complicated. All you have to do is come about suppertime, when he's eatin' over there at the nurses' station. All you have to do is keep him occupied for maybe thirty seconds. I'll go down the hallway like I'm goin' to take a leak. I'll close the hall door behind me. The exit door at the other end of the hallway is just locked with an allen wrench, and they leave it on the ledge above the door."

I am not speaking, but nodding my head rapidly up and down.

"They think that's a good place to hide a key. See what I mean when I say how simple it would be?"

"You mean I would help you escape. That's the favor you want me to do."

"Yeah, you listenin' to me at all, or what?"

"But what would you do after you escape from the hospital? Where would you go?"

"That's no problem; there are lots of places. All I need is to get on the road."

"But Luke, you don't have a car. How would you travel? Would you hitchhike?"

147

"No. No thumbin'. I'd go straight for the Iron Horse." He is smiling at me now with his white teeth. Why is he doing that? Has he seduced me like the voice warned?

The gleam in his eye frightens me, but I ask, "Please, what is the Iron Horse?"

Luke glances quickly at the security guard, who is still watching us. "Not so loud, okay?" He sits forward and says, "The Iron Horse is John's Harley. It's locked up in the garage over by his old apartment because the courts haven't decided what to do with his stuff. That's what happens when you die with no relatives. They just lock up all your stuff till the courts decide what to do with it."

"The Iron Horse is a motorcycle," I murmur.

"Yeah; the one Johnny was ridin' when he cracked up. It's got a twisted fender and some busted spokes, but I'm pretty sure it'll still run."

The audacity of his plan astounds me. So does its simplicity. *But how would I dare?* I have started to tremble; I lock my hands between my knees to make it stop.

Then the guard standing at the nurses' station says in a loud voice, "You got about one more minute, Luke."

"So what do you say?" Luke asks me quickly. "You wanna go for it?"

I'm so afraid. They have him locked up like a caged animal and the only thing plain to me is my own fear. "I don't think I could do it. How could I ever create a diversion?" The words catch in my throat.

He winces and says, "Your part is real simple, Red; all I'm askin' is a little distraction."

"But I just don't think I could." There are tears blurring my eyes but I refuse to let them come.

He says to me, "Either you can or you can't. There comes a time when you have to shit or get off the pot."

The guard is walking toward us, but I need more time. I stand up and whisper to Luke, "Please, I need more time. I have to think it over. I just need more time."

"That's cool," he says.

*

During crafts and through lunch I am somewhat groggy. I eat a few bites of tossed salad and drink my apple juice. If you chew and chew long enough, eventually it has to go down your throat. I'm still over a hundred pounds, it could be worse. I'm so afraid I will go flat out and become a useless lump at the very time Luke wants me to be resourceful.

In group I have dry mouth. We have a new member whose name is Antoinette; she is sitting in the mist. She has moved here from Chicago and her new house speaks to her with voices. I have a sky voice but she has a house voice.

Miss Dellapiano is sitting beside me; she asks me how many spices I can name. I can only think of origami, but I'm pretty sure that's a craft, not a spice. Anyway, we're supposed to be listening to Antoinette. She has so much static. I clamp my hands between my knees because I'm starting to get the shakes.

Luke wants me to help him escape from the hospital. At three-thirty I use the phone in the lounge to call my mother. I say to her, "I think I should come home now. I've been in the hospital long enough."

"Grace, we went through this the other night."

I speak to her coldly: "You do want me to come home and live with you, Mother. I am correct in assuming that."

"Of course I want you here, but I want you to get well so you can stay here. Have you brought this up with Dr. Rowe?"

My mother doesn't understand about the lump in my stomach; she doesn't know that Luke wants me to help him escape. "Dr.

149

Rowe says I'm not ready yet," I tell her. "She means well, but there's so much she doesn't understand; her life is so sound."

"We talked about a pass," Mother says. "Have you asked Dr. Rowe about a pass?"

"Yes, I have a pass. I can come home tomorrow for the weekend."

"Good. Let's take it one step at a time and trust Dr. Rowe."

She doesn't understand what Luke expects of me. "Mother, you are speaking in clichés."

"Maybe I'm a cliché kind of person, Grace. What else would you expect from a rock?"

Her sarcasm means I have hurt her feelings. "You always say my name when you patronize me," I tell her.

"I don't think that's fair."

"Mother, I have tears in my eyes. I'm not supposed to cry because I have mascara now."

"Grace, please. I'm trying to understand, but we have to follow Dr. Rowe's advice. We both need to trust her."

This is not going to work. I say goodbye and hang up the phone.

When six o'clock comes, I know I can't do it. I don't have the strength. I feel so woozy and shaky; I blame the stress. But I could never willfully create a diversion in order for Luke to escape.

My own cowardice is disgusting to me as always. Maybe I'm not lucid enough to be a real coward. It seems like my whole life is just a chain of panicky, disoriented states, linked one to the next. Something needs to be done but I am helpless. I could disappear from the face of the earth and not cause the tiniest blip or ripple.

First Luke terrified me and now I care for him. I have to tell him I can't do it; I can't just fail to show up without a word of explanation. It will be most humiliating, but I have to go back to the lockup wing and tell him I can't go through with it.

I'll need an excuse to go back on Luke's unit. The nurse will be

150

different on this shift, but I don't have time to get a written pass from Dr. Rowe. I go to the cafeteria and talk with the cook named Wilma Dean in the serving line.

"Please, if you don't mind, I'd like my gazpacho from the refrigerator."

"What's the matter, Grace? Not hungry tonight?"

She adds some remark about home cooking, then goes to the refrigerator. She returns with the mason jar of red soup. "You want this heated, Honey?"

"No, thank you, I'll just take the jar, please. I'm planning to share it."

I carry the cold jar in both hands and follow the yellow line, walking rapidly. What if the nurse won't let me give him the gazpacho? What if she sends me away? I lick my lips, but when I see the double doors of the lockup unit, I start to tremble. I'm afraid I'm going to get the shakes real bad.

I stand in front of the nurse's cubicle and she slides her panel as soon as she sees me.

Her tone of voice is curt when she asks me what I want.

The mason jar is clutched against my chest. "I brought some homemade gazpacho. I would like to share it with Luke."

"What is gazpacho? Do you have a pass?"

"Please, I don't have to stay and talk with him. May I just give it to him?"

"There is a procedure for visiting a patient on this unit."

I don't want to hear it all again. The shakes begin immediately and so do the tears. "My mother and I make it at home. We do it together. It's been approved by Mrs. Bonner. If I could just give it to him, then I would be happy to leave."

"I'll tell you what. Why don't you just leave it here with me? If I can get approval over the phone, I'll be happy to give it to him."

This is not going to work, and I am losing it. My heart is

151

palpitating and the flashbulbs are exploding. I can see Luke across the lounge, and the guard is walking toward me. "The mist will come," I say to the nurse. "The flashbulbs will blind me and the mist will come." Now all my words are caught in my throat.

The instant before I faint, I see more flashbulbs popping in the darkness, and then there is just the mist and the dark.

When I come to, I am lying in the soup and the broken glass. The ceiling tile has water stains. You notice things on your back. The nurse from the cubicle and another one I don't recognize are hovering over me, advising me to lie still. They are cloaked in the mist; their voices are far away. They are like Miss Shapiro in the parking lot.

They have a pillow for my head. This is very like a dream. The nurse I don't recognize is sponging gazpacho from my neck and arms with gauze pads and collecting shards of broken glass in her cupped hand.

"I hope it's not in my hair," I say. "Please tell me the gazpacho is not in my hair."

"Your hair is fine. There are some superficial cuts on this arm. Please lie still while we clean you up."

"I have processed my hair with shampoo and conditioner. It made a dramatic improvement in my appearance."

"You don't need to worry about your hair. Mrs. Grant is coming soon to take you back."

I twist my head so my eyes can search the room. The guard is not here, but neither is Luke. I'm certain he has escaped; I have created the diversion in spite of myself.

In my room, Mrs. Grant removes my soiled shirt and puts it in a hamper. There are bandages on my right arm. I lie on the bed while she fits the blood pressure cuff to my left arm. I think of Luke at large and my pulse begins to race.

"How are you feeling?" she wants to know.

152

"I'm a little woozy. The static is gone and so is the mist."

"Your pulse is rapid."

"Mrs. Grant, please tell me what happened."

"You fainted, and your mason jar broke."

"I mean with Luke. What happened to Luke?"

"He broke out." Mrs. Grant's lips are pursed with disapproval. "When everyone was fussing with you, he broke out."

"Something horrid will happen now, won't it? What will happen to him?"

"He'll be caught, only now he'll be in much more trouble than he was before. He had a violent row with the security guard."

I have seen his violence and I am suddenly short of breath. "Mrs. Grant, what violence? What happened?"

"I didn't see it, I only heard about it."

"Mrs. Grant, it really wasn't my fault. I only wanted to share the gazpacho with him."

"Of course it wasn't your fault." She asks me to sit on the edge of the bed, which I do. She takes my blood pressure again.

"Mrs. Grant, my heart is pounding and pounding. Is it possible for a person's heart to just pound itself to death?"

She smiles. "No, Grace, that isn't possible."

I am taking deep breaths and exhaling slowly. "You have to understand one thing," I say to her. "I would never, never do anything to hurt you."

"I know that, Grace. I don't think you're capable of hurting anyone. At least not on purpose. By the way, I don't think I've mentioned how nice your hair looks."

It is comforting having her here, but I can only think of Luke. Is there suffering because of me? I am getting the shakes again, so I clamp my hands between my knees.

"Mrs. Grant, I have no shirt on." My very small breasts have very pebbly gooseflesh.

"I know; I don't want you to get chilled." She puts away the blood pressure cuff and asks me if I'm still woozy.

"No, just chilled. Mrs. Grant, you are a kind and generous person. I would never do anything to hurt you."

"I believed that the first time you said it. Here." She sticks a thermometer in my mouth.

I speak clumsily with the thermometer in my mouth: "The Looney Tunes tee shirt please, and my uncle's fatigue jacket."

"I'm afraid you'll be too warm with the fatigue jacket."

"But I need it. Please."

She reads the thermometer and gives me some pills in the little plastic cup while I slip into the shirt and the jacket. "It's not time for my medicine, Mrs. Grant."

"Dr. Rowe is just increasing your Mellaril."

"I hope this doesn't mean I'm in trouble."

"Of course not."

"They used to give me Thorazine. Several times they changed my dosage. How long will I be on this increased dosage?"

"Not for very long, hopefully. Let's wait and see, okay?"

"Mrs. Grant, when you're a cuckoo bird, you are like a chemistry experiment. They put chemicals in your body and then observe the results."

She smiles at me. "Come on, Grace. Down the hatch."

After I take the pills I ask her, "It isn't my fault, is it?"

"If you mean about Luke Wolfe, of course it's not your fault. He's perfectly capable of messing up his own life all by himself."

"Please don't be too hard on him. He does have redeeming qualities." Luke asked me to help him escape. I did it in spite of myself. I'm afraid to tell her the whole truth. "But I would never cause anyone's suffering on purpose."

"I know that."

154

"I'm supposed to go home on pass tomorrow. Please tell me I still get to go."

"Of course you still have your pass. Why wouldn't you?"

She leaves me to rest and advises me to try and sleep. I try, but I have the shakes and my teeth are chattering. When I finally do fall asleep, I doze fitfully; no train comes, but I dream of the sticky, broken gazpacho and the flour on my mother's apron.

Nine

MOTHER WORKS THE edge of the mixing bowl with a rubber scraper while I drop the dollops of batter in straight rows on the cookie sheet. The hedges of Allerton are straight and regular like geometry. I wonder if Miss Ivey helped to make her birthday cookies in the hospital cafeteria. Her vibrating wrist would be like an electric mixer. I wonder where Miss Ivey is now.

"These are tollhouse cookies, Mother. We say chocolate chip, but their real name is tollhouse."

"I suppose that's true."

"I don't know who makes the rules about naming cookies. Whose authority is it? But you wouldn't offer someone a tollhouse cookie. You would offer them a chocolate chip cookie. You wouldn't find a Girl Scout going door to door selling tollhouse cookies."

My mother laughs.

I put the cookie sheet in the preheated oven, and I say to her, "As far as that goes, what is a tollhouse? I know what a *troll* house is, it's a place where a troll lives. But what is a tollhouse?"

Mother is smiling. "Where does all of this lead, Grace?"

"There are beginnings and endings but I can never locate them."

She wants me to go to her school with her to help decorate the gym for Halloween. I tell her I'd rather not.

"You might enjoy it, Grace. You could meet the other teachers."

"It's hard for me. People would know about me."

156

"They know you've been in the hospital, but they're very kind people. No one would make you feel uncomfortable."

"Ghosts and goblins and black and orange crepe paper."

"Yes, basically. A few staples and some Scotch tape."

I know my mother means well. "Not this time, Mother. I don't feel ready for it. I don't want to hurt your feelings."

She has put the mixing bowl to soak and is washing her hands. "My feelings aren't hurt, I just hate to see you miss out on things you might enjoy."

"I'll come another time. I'll spend some time writing in my journal while you're gone. Dr. Rowe wants me to keep it up."

"I might be gone most of the afternoon. Will you be okay?"

"I'm a little groggy because of the increased dosage. I think I'll be fine, though."

"You won't forget to take the cookies out? I've set the timer."

"I'll probably forget, but the timer will remind me."

After she leaves I take my journal and go to the balcony where the sun is weak against the chilly air. I cloak the old wool Navajo blanket around me like a cowl and wedge my chair back under the eaves. There are no towels draped over the railing.

I hope I'll be able to hear the timer from up here; it's very important. The scraggly Russian olive has lost all its leaves. It was forlorn when it had leaves, and now it's naked.

Then suddenly, I can think only of Luke.

Is he safe or is he captured? What will the authorities do to him when they capture him? If he does get away, will he spend his whole life running from predicaments? There was violence, I wonder if he is suffering; with my whole heart I hope not. I may never see him again; in fact, it's highly probable. It's so very, very odd, the sense of loss I feel.

I decide I'd better write these thoughts.

I take out the ballpoint pen and the doorbell rings. My heart begins a rapid pounding. I didn't see anyone approaching the apartment.

The doorbell is ringing and my mother is gone. I will have to answer it myself, there is no one else. What if the pounding turns to palpitations? Maybe the person will go away.

But it rings again and I rush downstairs. I crack the door and find that it is DeeDee. We hug each other and start talking. My cardiovascular system has returned to normal.

She wants to know how I'm doing.

"I think I'm doing better," I say. "I get a better night's sleep. I have learned the meaning of the train dream. Dr. Rowe has increased my Mellaril and sometimes I feel groggy."

"Are you home for good?"

"No, this is just a pass. I have to go back Monday. Dr. Rowe says I'm not ready to be discharged yet. Mother says we have to trust Dr. Rowe and take one day at a time."

"I'm so sorry about what happened to you, Grace. We never talked about it when Miss Braverman and I visited you."

She means about the Surlies. I look away.

"It was terrible what they did to you," she says. "It was horrible."

I can't look up. My stomach starts to swell. The halls at school are so long and there was the hot cigarette breath and there were hands tearing at my clothes. I swallow and take a deep breath.

"If MacFarlane found out, they would be expelled from school and they would probably go to jail. It's what they deserve. I don't want to butt in, Grace, but I would stand by you. It was DeWayne and Brenda and those hoods, wasn't it?"

I know she means well, but my stomach is twisted. "I can't say, DeeDee. I can't talk about this. Please, my mother asks me the same thing."

"I'm really sorry, Grace. You know how I open my mouth some-times. I'm really sorry. I don't want to say things that might hurt you."

I look up and her eyes are bright, as if she has tears forming. Her hair is so lovely. "I was sick and you visited me," I say. "You are a dear friend. You could never say anything wrong." This could be a special moment. I would like to reach out and touch her. Dr. Rowe says it would be okay, but I don't have the nerve. I wish I could tell her more, how much her friendship means to me, how much she teaches me about trust.

But she says, "Can I change the subject? I brought you this." She is giving me a folded piece of paper which turns out to be a handout on the science fair. I glance at the time of departure, the cost of meals, et cetera.

"You'll be out in time for the science fair, right? I hope so."

"I'm not sure. This is only a week from now. If I'm not out, I think Dr. Rowe would let me have another pass."

Then the timer goes off. It startles me. "The cookies are done," I say. "There are cookies."

I take the cookie sheets from the oven and set them on the coun-ter. DeeDee calls from the living room: "Do you need any help?"

"No, thank you. These are chocolate chip cookies. In a few minutes we can eat some."

"That sounds good to me."

I am looking and looking at the cookies. So much order in the rows that are so regular. "Chocolate chip cookies are tollhouse cook-ies," I call to her.

"I know."

The rows are straight as arrows, up or down or diagonal, no mat-ter which way you rotate the cookie sheets. So much geometry. And then I know, so suddenly and clearly it takes my breath away:

The hedges of Allerton. Luke is at Allerton Park.

159

It is vivid in my brain like a very sharp slide projected on a screen. He is at Allerton, in the sunken garden, where acoustics are so fine that sounds carry as easily as beams of light, where you can whisper at one end and be heard at the other.

I lean on the counter and begin deep breathing. He is at Allerton. How do I know this?

DeeDee is in the kitchen, with her hand on my shoulder. "Are you okay, Grace? What's the matter?"

"I think I'm fine. I need a few deep breaths and I'll be fine."

"You don't look fine. Sit down."

We sit at the kitchen table and I blurt it out with no introduction: "DeeDee, I know where Luke is. I know exactly where he is."

"It's like you're a million miles away. And who is Luke?"

"Who would think the knowledge could come from cookies?" As quickly as I can, I summarize about Luke and how he broke out of the lockup wing. I use my deep breathing to keep control.

"But you don't *know* he's there, you just think so."

"I know he's there. I'm certain as anything."

"How can you say that?"

"I can't explain it, I just know that he's there. It's amazing to me now. When I first met him I thought he was evil; he terrified me. I believed he was part of the Surly conspiracy. My voice warned me about him; that's the sickness. Maybe you know him — he goes to West High, or at least he used to."

DeeDee shakes her head. "I don't know him."

"The staff thinks he's a psychopath, but he's not; you have to know him beneath the surface. It's a tragic thing if a life is wasted because a person never gets a chance to be understood."

DeeDee says if I'm so certain where he is, I should call the hospital staff or the authorities so they can bring him back.

"Oh, DeeDee, I couldn't. He would be in so much more trouble. He needs to come back on his own, for the right reasons."

"What do you mean, the right reasons?"

"He has to trust somebody. He has to know that he can't spend his whole life running away from people in authority or rebelling against them. He has to know that everything will go better for him if he comes back on his own." I get one of the warm, soft cookies for myself and two for DeeDee.

"Let's say you're right, and he is there. You can't really be certain, but let's say you're right. What's the point?"

It's hard for me to believe the next words that come out of my mouth: "I want to go get him. I want to bring him back."

"What does that mean?"

"I can't force him to come back, I just want to convince him to come back on his own. DeeDee, please, I'm trying to ask you a huge favor. Would you drive me to Allerton?"

"That's almost two hours from here, isn't it?"

"Just about. It's so hard for me to ask for favors, DeeDee. I was pushy with the nurse on lockup. Please, I need this favor; I need to do this."

"I'm supposed to drive you down there and bring him back in my car? When I don't even know him and you told me he's violent?"

"Not bring him back, just drop me off. He wouldn't come back with someone he doesn't know anyway."

"Just drop you off? I'm sure."

"You don't have to worry, I'll be fine."

"You want me to drive you down there and leave you in the middle of nowhere? What kind of friend would I be?"

"It's not the middle of nowhere. I used to live there; I know all the grounds like the back of my hand."

DeeDee is shaking her head. "Why don't you ask your mother to help you?"

"My mother wouldn't understand. She wouldn't want me to go near him, not after what those people at school did to me. She

161

would call the hospital and tell them where to look for him, or she would tell me to forget it altogether. She would mean well, but that's what she would do."

DeeDee is munching on her cookie. "Grace, you don't know what you're asking."

"I do, though. Would you like another cookie?"

"No, thanks. Grace, this is such an impulse. Wouldn't it be a good idea to think it over for a day or two?"

I can feel tears forming in my eyes, but this is not the time for me to be crying. "Impulse is good for me. It may be the best thing possible. Besides, there isn't a day or two for thinking. It may be that Luke is hurt, and my pass is over tomorrow night."

"You say impulse is good for you. How am I supposed to know it really is? And I'm not saying that to hurt your feelings."

"I know. It grieves me to cause you this dilemma. The sickness brings so much data it paralyzes me. I can't act and I can't even think. The data comes all at once and I get scrambled. I wish I could explain it, but I can never find the words."

DeeDee doesn't say anything, but she is listening.

"When the voice comes it is worse, because it changes all the data. I know it's good for me to act, when I know what to do. I know Luke is there, and I believe I can help him."

"And what if he's not there? You don't think it's possible, but I do. Then what?"

"I would just stay overnight with Mr. and Mrs. Walters."

"Who are they?"

"They're the Allerton caretakers; they live right on the grounds, and they know me. I'm sure they would even bring me back home, if it turns out I need a ride."

"It isn't that I don't want to help you," she says, "but I don't know what to do."

My heart is in my mouth; maybe she's going to do it. Maybe she will drive me. To think it is exhilarating and terrifying at the same time. "I feel bad putting you in this position," I tell her, "but I really need to do this. I need to know the thing to do, and then do it." I know my eyes are bright with tears, but I'm not going to cry.

For the longest time DeeDee looks at me without speaking. She finally says, "If I do this, am I being a real friend to you, or am I betraying you?"

"You are being my friend because you are helping me do the thing that needs to be done."

*

The shiny Camaro whispers on the interstate like white noise. It's like riding on a cloud. DeeDee grips the steering wheel with both hands and gives the highway her undivided attention. I have given her a dilemma which is causing her much stress. I tell her I'm sorry.

"You don't have to apologize," she says, without looking away from the road.

"I know how you feel. Luke asked me to help him escape from lockup but I couldn't do it."

"The more you talk about him the more stressed out I get. Don't take it personally, but he sounds like a total hood. I don't like this feeling; I'm not used to it."

"I understand, DeeDee. I feel guilty for asking you and you feel guilty for taking me. We both feel guilty."

"It's not that I don't believe you. It's not that I think you're crazy."

"I know."

She is still looking exclusively at the road. She asks me if there will be people at Allerton.

"Not now. Not this time of year. They only have guests on holidays, once you get into October. But Luke will be there."

"You think. You hope."

I know she is not being quarrelsome, she is just expressing her conflict. "There are greenhouses at Allerton," I tell her. "They are run by the university. They grow all kinds of flowers there, even tropical ones. In the summers, my father worked in the greenhouses. He had hands that could mold a sculpture or nurture an orchid."

"You were really fond of him, weren't you?"

"Fond is one thing, but it's not good to be pathological. Dr. Rowe has helped me open my eyes. My father wasn't perfect. He could be impatient and he could be arrogant. It's important to know someone's imperfections and still love the person. When my dad died, he was cremated. The funeral home gave us the ashes in a brass urn, but I transferred the ashes to a clay pot my dad fired a long time ago. It's amazing that all of a person can fit into a pot no bigger than a Kool-Aid pitcher. I kept the pot next to my nightstand. Every morning I said my prayers beside it; I prayed for my father's soul, and Uncle Larry's, and anybody else I knew of who was suffering."

"But it must be disappointing that he was cremated; you don't have a grave to visit."

"I'm going to visit his grave now. That's where we're going."

"What do you mean, Grace?"

"I mean that his ashes are scattered at Allerton. He is part of the earth. In July, after we knew we were moving away, Mother and I went to the park one night. All the visitors have to leave at sundown. We had the urn with us."

"You scattered his ashes there," says DeeDee. "Why didn't you bring them with you to your new apartment?"

"Because Allerton was his place. My father and I explored every inch of the park together, at one time or another, in every season.

164

That's where he needs to be at rest. He is one with the earth; he is part of the soil that grows the wildflowers."

A tear is sliding down my cheek with no warning. I wipe it away quickly and glance at DeeDee to see if she noticed, but she is looking straight ahead. She seems rigid; I have given her information, but it hasn't eased her dilemma. All of a sudden I feel cold and numb. I look straight ahead at the pavement which slides underneath. Neither of us is speaking. It's as though the car is on automatic pilot, and DeeDee and I are a pair of robots.

When the huge cedar trees begin to line both sides of the narrow country road, I know we are near the entrance to Allerton.

"It's less than half a mile, DeeDee. The entrance is on the right." I can feel my pulse increase.

"Is that where I drop you off?"

"Yes, it'll be fine. I'll have to walk about half a mile on the service road, but I'll enjoy it. It will give me a chance to collect my thoughts."

"It's almost dark. I'll be dropping you off to walk in the dark."

"It won't be dark for a little while yet. Anyway, I know the park like the back of my hand, remember?"

"I remember everything; I still don't know why I'm doing this."

When we get to the service road entrance, the chain is pulled across and padlocked. I will have to walk around the pillars.

I get out of the car. "DeeDee, you remember your way back to the highway?"

"I remember."

"You're sure you remember every turn."

"I'm sure." She has both hands on the steering wheel. She speaks to me while the motor idles: "I'm going to call your mother as soon as I get back. I'm sorry, but I have to do it."

"We left notes, DeeDee. Don't forget we left notes. But if you

165

call her, it will make me happy. I don't want her to worry, and I don't want her to suffer."

"And promise you'll call me in the morning. It doesn't matter what time, you have to call."

"I promise."

"And I mean a solemn promise, not just an ordinary promise, and you have to call your mother too." DeeDee's eyes are bright with tears but she knows I don't mean to make her suffer.

When she leaves, I watch until the car is completely out of sight. I feel myself starting to shiver, so I button up the fatigue jacket.

I walk along the service road briskly until I come to the bridge which crosses the Sangamon River. The bridge forms a long and gentle arch. For a while, I lean against it and pick at the moist moss which grows from the cracks in its side. The quiet river wanders crooked into the timber; the sun sets and the moon rises. I feel strong inner peace. This is my place and my father's place; I have roots here.

About a quarter of a mile farther along, I find the path which cuts through the woods in the direction of the garden of the Fu dogs. The woods are dark and quiet. When I come abruptly out of the woods and stop in front of the first Fu dogs, I am losing breath but my legs are still firm. The Fu dogs sit on their tall pedestals. I know that they form two lines clear to the far end of the garden, clear to the pagoda of the Gold Buddha, although I can't see that far in the dark.

The way to the pagoda is a long black tunnel, formed by the arching dark trees. I walk as fast as I can, but the blue porcelain dogs form a gauntlet. The moonlight gleams on them where it slices through the trees; their fangs are bared like those of forest monsters. They are resentful because I am an intruder in the dark.

I try to walk faster but my legs are going wobbly. I can't do this if I'm scrambled. The gleaming eyes are boring into me on both

166

sides but I can see the silhouette of the pagoda. The Fu dogs are only porcelain; they can't have real eyes or real thoughts. They can't affect me because they have no affect.

I sit on the pagoda steps and begin some deep breathing. I have the shakes, but I will not be afraid of the gleaming blue dogs. My father is here; he permeates the soil like a nutrient.

When my breathing is restored and my legs are firm again, I follow the gravel path which leads through the formal gardens to the sunken garden. The uniform hedges are at right angles and diagonals. It isn't hard to see, there are pole lights and moonlight, but the shadows are deep. My feet are crunching the gravel and breaking the silence; I feel like a trespasser. But I tell myself not to be afraid, I have walked this path many times with my dad.

At the entrance to the sunken garden I sit on the steps; I breathe slowly, deeply, while my eyes adjust. The sunken garden is holy, dark, and deep; it is a fortress surrounded by concrete walls, a perfect oval hollowed in the earth, with a carpet of even grass. It has sanctuary purity.

But in a way, none of this seems real. What am I doing here? I'm waiting for Luke on this point in space and time. DeeDee was probably right. It does seem absurd.

I should probably be afraid. If Luke is here, and if he is truly a psychopath or one of the Surly People, then I am in real danger. There is no protection here. But I am not afraid. It is as if I have somehow moved to a zone deep inside myself where panic and fear are in orbit around me, but I am the calm eye of the storm. The source of this poise I know not.

It is a warm night for October but I am starting to feel chilled. The breeze rustles the leaves and branches scrape in the dark. I listen for the cattle. It would be a waste of time to listen for the mourning dove; she is not nocturnal. I wonder if her head is tucked beneath her wing.

167

Time goes by, maybe hours, I can't tell. Maybe I have slept. The moon is much higher and there are many stars. Then I hear the voice, quiet but clear.

"Hey Red. Over here."

For several moments, I hold my breath. It's Luke's voice.

"I said over here. Come on over."

I was right. He is here. My heart begins its pounding. My eyes are accustomed now and I can see him sitting on the grass, leaning back against the concrete wall.

I crouch onto my knees next to him. I can't speak yet.

"This is really far out, Red. What can I say?"

"I knew you would be here."

"How did you know that?"

"I'm not sure. I just knew. Sometimes you just know things." There is a large duffel bag next to him. He is wearing the headband but his hair is wild. Probably from highway wind, he did ride here on a motorcycle.

"You must have found the motorcycle," I say. "But where is it?"

"I stashed it in the woods. It was easier than I thought, gettin' it. They left a window unlocked in that garage. This duffel bag here belonged to Johnny; it was still strapped to the bike."

"I didn't mean to create the distraction," I say quickly. "I need to be honest. I was just coming to tell you I couldn't go through with it, and then I passed out."

He is grinning. "I figured it was somethin' like that. It worked anyway, though. The problem was, Old Four Eyes tackled me down by the exit door. I had to punch him out. I didn't want to, I've got nothin' against him personally, but he didn't give me no choice."

Is Luke apologizing to me? I have seen his violence yet I have chosen to be here with him. Alone. He could do anything he wants with me. He could break me like a stick or rip me with his huge organ. I'm sure I wouldn't think like this if I had my medicine. But I'm not even sure of that.

He asks me what time it is.

"I don't know. It's past midnight for sure, but it's not yet sunrise." I can feel my teeth chattering.

"I been sleepin' a lot since I got here," he says. "You're cold, Red, where's your stuff?"

"I don't understand."

"You came all the way down here and you didn't bring any stuff? You'll freeze your ass."

"I didn't think of it. This is Uncle Larry's fatigue jacket." I hug myself to stop the shivering but my teeth are still chattering.

Luke is unzipping the duffel bag. He takes out a leather jacket and hands it to me. "Put this on."

I put it on quickly. "I forgot my medicine too. I left it at home because I left in such a hurry."

"Is that a problem?"

"It might be or it might not be. I don't know for sure. This is a very disorienting situation, but when it comes to the medicine I'm never sure. It's scary to be without it. Whose coat is this?"

"It was Johnny's. That's what I'm sayin', his duffel bag was still strapped to the bike and a lot of his stuff was still in it."

My teeth are chattering and I'm wearing the too-big coat of a dead man. "My father is here. This is a special place."

"It's a real nice place, Red, and it's real good for hidin' out. But you told me your old man was dead."

"His ashes are scattered here. He was cremated. When you're part of the soil that nurtures living things, you're never really dead."

Luke shifts his weight. He has perspiration on his face, I wonder why. "Red, you didn't go to all the trouble of findin' me just so you and me could shoot the shit."

169

"I came to talk you into coming back." There, I said it.

"You want me to go back and let them lock me up again?"

"Please don't put it that way, there's more to it than that. Dr. Rowe will help you, I know she will."

"You want me to turn my life back over to the bullshitters?"

"Please don't twist it, Luke. Dr. Rowe is not a bullshitter. She's real understanding and I know you can trust her. She will help you, really."

"It isn't just her, Red. We're talkin' about the whole system. How did you get here?"

I tell him how DeeDee brought me. "She's my friend. I gave her the dilemma but she brought me anyway."

"Does anybody else know you're here?"

"Just DeeDee and my mother. I didn't tell the hospital or anybody in authority. I want you to come back, but it has to be for the right reasons. You have to choose to come back."

Suddenly his hand is on mine. "It took guts for you to come, Red. I want you to know I appreciate that."

"It was an impulse. There must be constructive impulses and destructive ones; it only stands to reason."

"But I've got to be free and clear. Life doesn't work for me like it does for other people, not with the bullshitters in charge. I tried to explain all that to you."

"But Luke, Dr. Rowe says your life won't work until you learn to make appropriate decisions."

"You know how many times I've heard that, from one bullshitter or another?"

"Please, I don't mean to be quarrelsome. I just want you to trust me."

"I do trust you. You're real different, but I respect the way your mind works."

"I can't think of anything more ironic; the way my mind works is

170

pathological most of the time. But this time I know what's right. It will be best for you to come back of your own free will."

"The thing is, I know your heart's in the right place. I know in your own mind, you're tryin' to look out for me. I don't want to put you down. You understand what I'm sayin'?"

"Yes. You're saying that even if you don't take my advice, I'm not to take it personally; you know that I care about you as a human being."

"You got it."

"Luke, please. The point is, if you don't come back, they will find you. Eventually they will find you. When they do, the consequences will be much worse." I'm wearing two jackets, why are my teeth still chattering?

"It's easy for you to say. You haven't spent your life with the bull-shitters on your back."

I am shaking my head back and forth rapidly. "It's never easy for me to say, not if I have to convince someone of something. I just know that things will work out better for you if you come back voluntarily. Somebody will show leniency. Even Mrs. Grant says so. I'm sure you know Mrs. Grant."

"In a way, I'd like to believe you." The sweat is still beaded on his forehead; it's so chilly, why is he sweating? "When I'm eighteen, I'll be free and clear for sure. The system can't touch me then."

"But Luke, you can't just be on the run until your eighteenth birthday. Things like that have a way of adding up. Please, I'm no good at this, you have to help me. It's wise for you to come back; aren't you going to listen to me at all?"

"I already *am* listenin' to you. I told you that once."

I am chilled clear down to the bone. "Luke, I have to go to the bathroom real bad."

"That's cool, life goes on."

171

I hug myself to stop the shivering but my teeth are still chattering. "If I could go, I wouldn't be so cold. I have to go real bad."

"Go in the woods. You only have to take a leak, right? It's dark and there's nobody around. I won't look at you, I promise."

It won't be easy, but I'm shivering so hard I either have to do as he says or wet my pants. "Are you sure?"

"I'm sure. It's no sweat."

I walk up the steps and into the woods, crunching sticks and leaves, until I find a spot that seems private enough. The moonlight is bright and many trees are bare. I squat down and the weeds are scraping my haunches. It's a few moments before I can actually go; then I wish Luke would make some noise, the stream seems so loud it's embarrassing. In the pockets of the jacket, I find old Kleenex which I use for wiping.

I am back and Luke is on his feet. "You feel better now?"

"I feel much better now," I say. "But have you thought about what I said?"

"I'm on my feet, right?"

"What does this mean?"

"It means we're goin' back. We're gonna try it your way."

All of a sudden I have a lump inside which is euphoric. He's coming back. He trusts me. "I'm so glad, Luke. You won't regret this."

"I already do. I'll tell you what the point is, Red. You knew where I was, you could of told the bullshitters. But you didn't; what you did took guts."

Can it be this easy? I did the right thing. "I tried to explain it to DeeDee. It's very hard to believe in impulses, especially when you're not used to having them."

Luke turns to pick up the duffel bag and he grunts. It is a grunt of pain, as if he's had a punch to the stomach. "You're hurt," I say suddenly. "Where are you hurt?"

"In my left leg. It's nothin' serious, I'll be fine."

"But how did it happen?"

"It happened between me and Four Eyes. We busted up some glass in a cubicle."

"Oh no. I knew where you were and I knew you were wounded. It came to me crystal clear."

"Forget it. I told you I'll be fine." He has the duffel bag over his shoulder.

I understand his perspiration now and I'm afraid for him. "What are we going to do next?" I ask.

"We said we're goin' back, right? Let's go get the Iron Horse."

He means to drive us back on the motorcycle, and I've never even sat on one. "But you're hurt; how could you drive? We don't have to go now, we can wait until it's light. I can call my mother or DeeDee to come and get us — I can use the caretaker's phone."

He is shaking his head. "No way."

"But why?"

"Nobody's *takin'* me back. If I'm goin' back, I'm goin' the same way I came. On the bike."

"But your leg —"

"Forget about my leg, it doesn't matter. The point is, your mother knows where you are. That means she knows where *we* are."

My teeth are still chattering lightly and my heart is thumping. Why did I think it would all be easy, once the decision was made? I say to Luke, "I know what you're saying. She will call the authorities; she won't have any choice."

"I'm no expert, but I think that's how mothers do things. If there's any cops comin', I want to get the hell out of here now. No bullshitter is takin' me back."

I have to swallow hard and breathe a little. I can understand his point. He has trusted me, so I should trust him now. "Okay," I say meekly.

173

The trees are dark walls lining our path; we walk a hundred yards or so on the crunchy gravel to a service exit on the other side of the sunken garden. We are walking slowly; part of the time he leans on my shoulder.

Even in the dark, the motorcycle is black and gleaming. Just barely, I can make out a flared gold eagle on the gas tank. Luke grips the handlebars and yanks it forcefully onto the shoulder of the roadway. He grunts his pain.

"It must be so heavy," I say.

"Liftin' it on one leg, it's heavy," he says. He is short of breath. I feel so helpless. It grieves me that he is in pain, but I must let him do it his way. He climbs onto the seat and kicks down twice with his right leg. The motor roars to life, very very loud.

Luke is grinning now. "This is the Iron Horse," he says in a loud voice.

The Iron Horse scares me. I have never been on a motorcycle in all my life. I tell him it's very nice, even though I wouldn't know a nice motorcycle from a not-nice motorcycle.

"What? Speak up!"

"It's very nice!" I say, louder. There is no static, but so much motor noise. Will we be conspicuous, making so much noise in this quiet place? Luke has both feet on the ground to hold the bike upright.

The motor is blubbering. He is wearing a leather jacket and putting on a tight wool stocking cap; his long hair trails below like streamers. He hands me leather gloves and a green wool stocking cap from the duffel bag. "Put these on," he says.

I put them on quickly.

"These are Johnny's too," he says loudly. He is strapping the duffel bag to a metal frame above the taillight.

"Aren't we supposed to wear helmets?" I ask.

174

"Helmets suck. They're for wimps. Climb on, Red, the road's callin'."

His enthusiasm is a side of him I haven't seen. Even with the pain he must feel. I climb on behind him slowly, and he tells me, "We're gonna stay on back roads; you know, county blacktops and like that."

I nod my head rapidly up and down, but I don't speak. He gives me instructions, which I am able to hear over the noise because our heads are close together: "Put your feet on the pegs and hold on tight. You're safe, you got the sissy bar behind you."

I clutch the sides of his jacket tightly with both hands.

"When we go into turns, you have to lean your body into the turn. It's safer that way because it keeps the bike balanced."

"I'm scared to think about the turns."

"It's only a little scary until you get used to it, and then it's a lot of fun. You'll see, everything is cool."

There is a little static popping his voice. "I left my mother a note," I say. "I hope I'm not causing her to suffer."

"That's not my department," he says, with his widest smile. "I don't know anything about mothers. Besides, I'm a psychopath, remember?"

Then there must be a look on my face because he says, "Chill out, Red, you're gonna dig it."

The motor roars suddenly and shakes. We leap forward with no warning, spinning gravel and throwing it up behind. My heart is in my mouth. We are whizzing along the blacktop and swerving suddenly to avoid the speed bumps. It is like I am flying through space with every connection to the earth cut. If I had time to think, surrendering to him like this would panic me. The wind is so strong and so loud and so cold.

We are flying out of Allerton and into the dark. The dark is the abyss, why couldn't we stay longer? The abyss is black and cold, but I absolutely mustn't get scrambled, not on the back of a whizzing Iron Horse. The wind is roaring in my ears. Luke's back seems big and strong as a brick wall. I close my eyes and grip his jacket with all my might and press my head between his shoulder blades.

Ten

LUKE CALLS THIS place a roadhouse. It is a bar, a restaurant, a grocery store, and a poolroom, all under one roof. The lighting is dim. The dark wooden booths are empty, except for the one where we are sitting. On the floor next to the juke box there is a metal bucket which looks like it's meant for catching drips.

Behind the bar there is a long horizontal mirror but it's hard to look in it because it's recessed and because of all the lined-up liquor bottles. There is a transparent sphere Budweiser clock which hangs at the end of a gold chain from the ceiling above the bar. The clock rotates with little pops of light; it is the eye in the sky. The eye in the sky sees everything, but this is not the sky. If the sky has an eye, then whose eye is it, is it God's? My father and I made many God's Eyes. *Ojo de Dios.* It's not good for me to think this way; maybe I need my medicine.

"This place is great," says Luke. "There's no tellin' what you'll find when you go on the road."

I don't know why we need to loiter here, but Luke says he is very hungry and he also says we need to take the time to enjoy being on the road. We rode until it was dawn, stopping once while Luke siphoned some gas from a car parked on a side street in a tiny town. The road and the miles whizzed by, but I was lost in the dark and the dark was the abyss. We were whizzing into the abyss. My body is stiff and I am so tired. My head is thick and my eyes are burning. When I turn my head, the objects I look at have little trailers

177

of popping lights like the spots that linger after flashbulbs. Luke says it's probably just fatigue; he may be right, who knows?

"You need some breakfast," he says.

"Please, I'm not hungry. You must know by now what my appetite is like."

"Then drink your coffee. You can't do this without a little caffeine."

"But Luke, I don't like coffee."

He shrugs. He is eating scrambled eggs and American fries. I look at the bar where two men in coveralls are drinking coffee. The waitress has a hairnet, lots of red lipstick, and is smoking a cigarette. She is standing directly beneath the eye. She does not control the eye, but the eye may control her; I'm not sure.

Next to the bar is a pay phone. "Maybe I should call my mother."

Luke's mouth is full. "Go ahead. Tell her we're comin' back, but don't tell her where we are."

"How could I? I don't know where we are."

He shrugs and keeps chewing. I call DeeDee. She is so relieved to hear from me; she thanks me for keeping my promise. I tell her everything is okay and we're on our way back.

"DeeDee, please do me a favor and call my mother. Please tell her what I've told you."

"But you said you were going to call her."

"DeeDee, please. I'm out of quarters and the waitress here is curt. She makes me uncomfortable." I'm very careful not to mention the eye.

"Okay, I will. But come home right away. *Please.*"

"Thank you, DeeDee."

When I get back to the booth, I take a sip of the bitter coffee Luke has ordered for me and I feel an acid turn in my stomach.

"How do you feel?" he wants to know.

"It's important that I've contacted my mother; I don't want her to

178

suffer. I feel a little numb. Sometimes I get too numb to be scared."

"You need to mellow out," he says.

"I can't go flat out, though. That's one thing I absolutely can't let happen."

Luke is finished with his breakfast. He is drinking coffee. He smiles his wide smile and lights a cigarette and says, "After you put away that first breakfast, then sit back and light up, that's when you know you're truly on the road."

"I don't understand." I try just a little bit more of the coffee.

"On the road means out from under. Back in June, when me and John went on the road, we rode all night the first night, then in the morning we stopped at a truck stop someplace in Michigan. We had eggs, and toast, and bacon, and after we finished eating, we both lit a cigarette and kicked back. It was at that exact moment that I felt like I was closin' a door behind me. I don't think I could explain it to you, Red. I felt free and clear like I'd never felt before. With this big grin on his face, John said to me, he says, 'Welcome to the road, Luke.'"

"You were on your way to do migrant work. Migrant work would scare me; there's no support system."

"No bullshitters, you mean. And if you want the truth, on the road doesn't always mean you have a destination. It just means out from under. The way John used to say it was, if you stand too long in one place, the system will claim you. If the system claims you, you will spend your life against the flow. I didn't understand all of it, but at least I knew what he meant by the system; he meant the system of bullshitters which runs your life. The truth is, I didn't even understand why he wanted me around. He was so much older than me. He told me once he thought I had a good mind. I couldn't believe it, it was the only time anybody ever told me that."

Luke is blowing smoke rings in the still, dim air. My eyes are

179

burning from weariness, not from the smoke. "I can't believe I'm here doing this," I say. "I've never been away from home except for the times in the hospital."

"I keep tellin' you to mellow out."

"I would hate to be away from home alone. I know how resourceful you are, but sometimes you scare me. Please don't be offended."

He is putting out his cigarette. "It's no problem. You heard what I was tellin' you about me and John. There's one thing I wish I knew." His dark eyes are suddenly glittery, like mica. They are mirrors, and I am in his eyes again, only double, like tiny twins.

I'm uncomfortable, but I ask him what the one thing is. He says, "I'd just like to know if John was truly my friend."

"How do you mean?"

"I hate to admit this, but I don't think I ever had a real friend. Not a real one. Not movin' every year or two from one group house to the next one, not with your basic weirdos and misfits. You know what I mean? I hate to put it this way."

"I think I understand."

"Here's what I'm gettin' at. Whenever I think about pullin' John's plug, and if it was right or wrong, it seems to come down to, were we really friends? Don't ask me why, it just seems more important than what I actually did."

The way he asks the question is very moving, but I am looking at my tiny selves in his glittery eyes. "I think he asked for your help when he was dying, and you were willing to help him. In fact, you were willing to take a risk to help."

"Yeah, Red, but that's what I already know."

"Please, I'm used to *needing* insight, not giving it. In my opinion it means you were the best friend John could have and probably the best friend he did have. I don't think you want to hear this, but it might be a good question to ask Dr. Rowe."

He turns his face away quickly. "I don't want the opinion of a bullshitter, I just want yours."

I can feel my pulse starting to race but I say, "Please, Luke, I've tried to tell you that Dr. Rowe is not a bullshitter."

"What difference does it make?"

"I think maybe it makes a big difference. I'm not very good at this, but you told me about pulling John's plug. When you were able to see pulling his plug as an act of rebellion, you were able to make your decision. If you make rebellion a way of life, you can't really be free; you can't really make your own choices."

"You're way over my head, Red, and besides, I thought we were talkin' about Dr. Rowe."

"But I don't think I *am* over your head, Luke. If you don't see people, if you only see bullshitters, all you will ever do is react. I remember when you threw the tables over in the cafeteria. Rebelling against authority is reacting, and reacting isn't choosing. Authorities will make decisions and you will react. Instead of making real choices, you will only react to the ones *they* make. It seems like freedom, but it's really not."

Luke looks at me and lights another cigarette. I wish he wouldn't ask me to do things I'm no good at; he wants my opinion and then he expects me to defend it. My face must be giving me away because he says, "Don't feel bad. I asked you and you told me."

"I don't think I've ever spoken to a person this way before. I can't imagine how judgmental I must sound."

"You have an amazing mind," he says. "You go real deep."

"I wish I could explain things as well as my father could, he always said when you protest it has to be because you're *for* something, not against. You have to be *for* something. I want you to understand, Luke, but I would never hurt your feelings. My own life is such a mess, how would I dare to criticize another person?"

181

"Like I say, you apologize too much. This is food for thought."

Then he tells me he needs to go to the bathroom and get cleaned up.

He leaves me sitting by myself. I hope and hope I haven't hurt his feelings. The waitress comes to ask me if I want more coffee, but my cup is still half full. She doesn't understand that I am not a coffee drinker, but how could she?

I should call my mother. I made DeeDee do it. I could get some change at the bar.

I hope Luke won't be gone long. How can it be that he is now such a source of reassurance? The eye is rotating. Of course it is only a spherical Budweiser clock but a rotating eye has a total field of vision.

Then two policemen come in laughing, in brown uniforms. They are middle-aged and overweight and hitching their belts. Nothing would ever intimidate them. I watch their epaulets and their sidearms, but the light pops; I swallow hard. They sit at counter stools eating doughnuts and drinking coffee and talking to the waitress. They are sitting directly beneath the eye. I wonder if they are state troopers.

From time to time they look at me. Do they look at me because they know I am helping a fugitive or only because there is no one else to look at? All of a sudden my breathing is tight.

I don't believe the policemen have knowledge of me, but they are sitting beneath the eye. If they get control of the eye, I will be helpless; they will know everything. Don't forget, it's just a clock, it's delusional thinking which makes it a rotating eye. Everything has trailers of light. This shouldn't be happening, do I have to backslide this way? If I don't get away from this booth, the shakes are coming. I may even get scrambled.

I stand up and walk rapidly out the door. There are gas pumps. I go around to the side of the building where the bathrooms are.

The women's has a cardboard OUT OF ORDER sign on the door. My breath is so short I have no choice; I knock loudly on the door of the men's room.

I hear Luke's voice say "It's open," but I knock again anyway.

"Please, Luke, it's Grace. May I come in?"

"I said it's open."

I step inside quickly, close the door behind me, and lean against it. The light is dim. There is a small sink. On the other side of the metal stall partition, Luke is urinating. I lean hard against the door.

"I'm awfully sorry, Luke."

"No problem, what's the matter?"

"This is unfair of me. You deserve your privacy."

"I told you it's no problem. What's the matter?"

His urine is plunging into the toilet in a loud and steady stream. Can a man pee so much? I'm quite sure his large organ is out and he is holding it. I won't move, but there's no reason to be afraid. I tell him quickly about the two policemen.

"What it probably is is a couple of local sheriff's deputies. I doubt if they can find their ass with both hands."

"They were looking at me."

"No other chicks to look at, right? Don't worry about it." Then he changes the subject. He says, "Hey Red, check this out. There's an eight hundred number on this spare roll of toilet paper. It says here if you have any questions or comments you should call this toll-free number."

I'm not sure how to react to the toilet paper data, but at least I'm not so lightheaded. Luke has flushed the toilet and is emerging from the stall. He begins washing his hands. "Is that prime or what? What bullshitter thought that one up, you s'pose? I'm sure I'm gonna call an eight hundred number and have a conversation about a roll of asswipe."

The idea of phosphates occurs to me, but the way he says it seems funny; I begin to giggle.

"It can get real gritty and funky on the road," he tells me. He goes on to say that it helps your morale to keep yourself cleaned up. He takes off his shirt and begins to scrub his torso with soap and water. His muscles are well defined and I find myself looking at his skin.

I am embarrassed but at least I have stopped giggling. I step inside the stall and close the partition door. "Luke, how am I supposed to clean up? I don't have any bathroom items."

"Do what I'm doin'. Take off your shirt and wash up."

Take off my shirt? What does this mean?

"I'll loan you some stuff. I've got lots of extra supplies. I've got an extra washrag here."

He passes me a hot, wet washcloth over the top of the partition door, along with a small bar of Ivory soap.

I'm sure it must be good advice. I take off the fatigue jacket, but it seems like a long time before I find the nerve to finally take off the Looney Tunes tee shirt.

I put both shirts on top of the dusty toilet tank. I am naked to the waist; it feels so vulnerable. Luke is only three feet away, splashing in the sink and brushing his teeth. If Luke saw me at this moment would he find me arousing or would he be indifferent? Which would be worse? It would be so embarrassing. It feels like such a scary situation, but I know I don't have to fear him. DeeDee feeds the fish in her underwear; I wonder if she enjoys knowing that males are aroused by her large and shapely breasts, or is it a matter of no interest to her?

I resume my breathing and begin washing with the soapy cloth. I remember immediately why I don't shave my armpits; I have prickly stubble.

184

When I mention it to Luke, he passes me his Bic razor. "You can use this. It's pretty sharp. You can use the soap for lather."

I shave slick and clean. My tee shirt has B.O. so I decide not to wear it. I roll it up and put on the fatigue jacket by itself; the coarse material is scratchy on my nipples, but I need the ventilation.

"I need to brush my teeth but I don't have a toothbrush."

He says, "You can use mine."

Can you share another person's toothbrush? The idea is repulsive to me, but if I said so it would only hurt his feelings, so I decide to say nothing. He continues, "I'll sterilize it for you. I'll scrub it with soap and water. It'll be like a toothbrush that just came out of the box." At times it seems like he can read my mind.

Anyway, Luke says the road has different rules. He has gotten us this far and he has made the right choice. I need to trust him. I run a comb several times through my hair and scrub my face.

Before we leave, I brush my teeth.

*

The gravel pit seems like a desert, especially on this day of hazy Indian summer heat. There's no moisture here, and nothing growing except a few pitiful weeds. The piles of gravel look like dunes reaching into the distance. It seems like another planet or another world. It would be easy to get lost among the piles; they all look the same and there are no lines to follow.

I ask Luke why we have stopped here. I tell him it's important to get back to the hospital.

He is drinking warm wine from a large bottle and eating pretzels. "What's the rush? We'll get back soon enough."

"I wonder how your leg is."

"That's another thing. I need to rest the leg."

I'm afraid for him, I wonder how bad his wound is. When we get back to the hospital, the staff can heal him. He gives me a banana which I eat slowly. He wants to give me driving lessons on the Iron Horse, but I tell him I never could.

"How do you know unless you try?"

"I could never drive a motorcycle, I wouldn't know the first thing about it. Don't you think we need to get back to the hospital?"

"You know your problem, Red? You need to take a chance every once in a while."

"I took a chance by coming to Allerton to find you. It scares me to take risks. I don't have my medicine. I have no experience with motorcycles."

"You just spent several hours on the bike. All you're gonna do now is move up to the front seat and drive. Come on, Red, live a little." He takes another bubbling swallow of the wine.

Before I know it, Luke has kick-started the bike. I am straddling the front seat and gripping the vibrating handlebars. He is behind me, on the passenger's seat. His strong hands are on my waist.

The motor is too loud. "To tell you the truth, Red, there's not a hell of a lot I can do from back here. I can't reach the handlebars to help with the controls, so you're gonna be basically on your own. 'Bout all I can do is use my feet to help keep the bike standin' up." He is shouting. His sweet, winey breath is hot on my neck.

I am scared. I release the kickstand and suddenly the bike is so terribly heavy it seems more than I can do to just hold it upright.

When I tell him so, he only says, "That's because it's standin' still. I'll help you keep it up. There's no weight at all hardly once it's in motion."

He reviews all the basics loud in my ear, but why do I have to try this? Aren't we supposed to be on our way back to the hospital? The throttle is right and the gearshift is left. The front brake is the right handbrake and the rear brake is the right foot pedal. You shift with your left toe and be sure you don't rest your leg against the tailpipe.

I shift into first and turn up some throttle. We are surging forward and it's scary. I can't help myself, I turn back on the throttle and the motor kills. The bike is so heavy I can't hold it up; it topples to the left and something hard and sharp is gouging painfully into the calf of my leg. I yank with all my strength to get the Iron Horse upright again. Luke is grunting and cursing and gripping at the seat beneath me.

He gets off quickly, puts down the kickstand, and kick-starts the motor once again. "Everybody kills it when they're just learnin'," he says. "Don't back off the throttle when you're movin'. Stayin' in motion is the secret. Try it again." The perspiration is beaded on his forehead and on his temples.

"Please, Luke, do I have to?"

"Don't be scared. You can do it."

I try again with the same result. Luke jumps off immediately, starts the bike, and gives me more advice.

We try it a third time and a fourth time, but I can't do it. My leg hurts and there are tears stinging my eyes. It is so frustrating. Why am I in an alien gravel pit trying to drive a motorcycle?

"Please, Luke, I can't do it." The tears are running down my face.

"Goddamit, Red, don't quit."

"But I just can't."

"That's bullshit. Keep tryin'."

The throttle is right and the gearshift is left. The front brake is the right handbrake and the rear brake is the right foot pedal. You shift with your left toe and be sure you don't rest your leg against the tailpipe.

Again and again, but he won't let me quit. Is this his secret, that

187

he just takes life by the throat? I find myself suddenly getting angry, but who or what is the target of the anger?

Finally, I have the bike in motion and keep it there. I have made it into second gear and we are cruising at a moderate pace. I am doing this. It's a little scary, making the curves around the gravel piles, but I manage. I throttle up a little bit and we are moving faster. I feel in control. Motion is my ally. It is frightening but also exhilarating, like learning to fly. My leg still hurts, but what if my father could see me now?

I am doing this.

Before we shut down the bike altogether, Luke tries to teach me to kick-start it, but with only partial success.

Then we do shut the bike down, and Luke says this calls for a celebration. He is limping severely. We hollow ourselves a comfortable niche in the base of one of the gravel piles. We are passing the wine back and forth. I am taking small sips but he is taking his long, bubbling swallows. It is the first time I have had wine except from the glass of one of my parents.

Luke has lit another cigarette. "I knew you had it in you, Red; you are a bad-ass momma." He seems to be getting a little drunk.

"I'm glad I did it," I say, "but you are achieving an altered state."

He laughs. "I'm gettin' a little looped, I guess."

"It seems like the recent years of my life have been one continuous altered state. But it frightens me if you get drunk; how will you drive the motorcycle? We need to be getting back to the hospital."

"There's no rush, Red, chill out a little bit."

"Luke, don't call me Red. Please call me Grace."

"Okay. Grace. I'm sorry, I didn't mean any disrespect." He seems to be having trouble with his breathing.

"It's okay. Please tell me why you taught me to drive the bike."

"I just thought it would be a good idea. It's a good thing for a person to know how to handle a bike."

188

Now I feel that reality is dawning on me. I knew it couldn't be this easy. "That's not the real reason, is it?"

He looks away and closes his eyes. "I wanted to give you something."

"I guess I must be an idiot or I would have understood sooner. You wanted to give me something because we won't be seeing each other anymore. You're not going back with me, are you?"

"I can't do it, Red. Grace, I mean. Now that we've got this far, you can get back on your own easy. Use the phone at the roadhouse. Your mother or your friend can get down here in less than an hour."

"But what will happen to you?" I ask. I feel hollow inside.

"Me and the Iron Horse will be on the road. I'll be free and clear." His words are coming through clenched teeth. He has so much sweat.

"That's the real reason you made sure we left Allerton. That's the real reason we're here at this gravel pit. You never meant to go back with me."

"Don't take it personal, Grace. I'm real sorry I had to lie to you."

There are tears sliding down my face. "Teaching me to drive a motorcycle is not a real gift. If you want to give me a real gift, come back to the hospital with me."

"There's one thing that wasn't a lie: I really do appreciate how you put yourself out for me. I can't remember when anybody cared about me that much. I won't forget it."

I know he's telling the truth; he has far too much conscience to be a psychopath. But he's trembling. I reach over and touch his face. He is soaking wet and very warm. "You've got a fever," I murmur.

"I'll be okay," he says.

My fingers travel above his left knee to a place where his jeans are wet and sticky. "You're bleeding."

"I said I'll be okay."

The knife he used for peeling the fruit is on the ground beside

189

him. I use it and begin slitting his pants leg from mid-calf up the inseam. It's slow going because it's so difficult to saw through the heavy denim and still be careful that the knife won't make contact with his skin.

"Oh God no."

Blood. There is so much blood. Some of it is dried and caked, but most of it is fresh, flowing from the long and deep gash in his thigh. I have to catch my breath. I take the deepest breaths I can. So much blood. There was blood in the bathtub, it flowed like a river of red.

"This is the wound," I say. "This is the wound from fighting with the security guard. There was blood; I asked Mrs. Grant if there was blood but she didn't know."

He doesn't speak. He seems so passive now. I go on, "This was starting to heal. You opened it up again when you were teaching me to drive the bike."

He doesn't answer but he doesn't have to. I know what happened and I know I have to be strong or he will die. I am still breathing hard with a rapid pulse, but I have found a calm center somewhere.

"You can go," he says, in a hoarse voice. "All I have to do is rest a little while and I'll be okay."

"You think you can drive the motorcycle, don't you? You can't even think properly; you've lost so much blood you aren't getting enough oxygen to your brain."

"A little rest and I'll be okay."

It frightens me to look at the gaping, flowing wound but I have to act. "This is absurd. Luke, you have no idea, do you? If we don't go back to the hospital, you're going to die from loss of blood."

"I have the Iron Horse."

"You have to listen to me. If you don't do what I say, you're going to die. You have to listen to me."

190

He has the sweats and the shakes. "Jesus Christ, I'm gettin' cold. I'm about to freeze here."

I help him squirm into his leather jacket and I zip it up. "You're cold because you have fever. That means you have infection. I'm not asking you, I'm telling you. We're going back."

He moves his head up and down several times. I guess it means yes. There is still the bleeding. I have to do what needs to be done or he will die.

"Do you have a belt?" I ask him.

"Why do you care if I have a belt?" he wants to know.

"Because there has to be a tourniquet." I am taking off my fatigue jacket. I wind it and twist it into a ropelike shape and then wrap it in a tourniquet around his upper thigh. I am naked to the waist, but the bleeding has to be stopped. "You have to understand," I tell him.

"I said I'd go back," he says. He is shivering with chills. His words come through clenched teeth.

"It's not enough if you're only going back because you're too sick to do anything else. All those things we talked about at the roadhouse. You have to understand."

"I don't understand things fast. I'll work on it."

I am getting the knot tied, but it's difficult, I have to be careful not to hurt him. It takes an anchor to make a good tourniquet. There is a stick on the ground which seems strong enough. When the stick is tied into the tourniquet, I twist it tight; it has to stop the bleeding. "I want you to understand the point. That's all I want."

He shakes his head rapidly up and down. I guess it means yes. I tuck the slit pants leg into his sock as carefully as I can, so it won't gap open too much when we're riding.

I am done and I get to my feet. I'm a little lightheaded, but I take some deep breaths. "You think you can be free and clear on a

191

bike that's stolen," I say to him. Then I realize I'm preaching at him and I have to stop it, especially when he's down so bad. It's taking advantage, and I should be ashamed.

He interrupts my thoughts: "Hey, Red."

"What?"

"Nice tits."

"Stop it. You're practically dying, and you choose to make a smart remark."

He is smiling, as much as he can through the chills. "I guess I gotta be me."

My tee shirt and the leather jacket are both in the duffel bag on the bike. The weather is hot, but I've got chills; I put them both on quickly.

The two of us are very clumsy, the way we stumble to the bike and climb on. It doesn't seem real when I take the handlebars and he sits slumped behind me; it seems like "Let's Pretend." Luke has his arms around my stomach; his fingers make a tight grip on the folds of my jacket.

The bike is so heavy and I've never started one before on my own. I straddle it, shaky, and try to kick the motor over. I kick down with all my might but I am too shaky. The bike is going to fall over; I am going to fail because the panic is coming.

Oh God no. If I can't do this, Luke will die.

Of course I could walk to the roadhouse; it can't be more than four or five miles. I could walk to the roadhouse and phone for help. My mother would come in the car or DeeDee would come. I am starting to cry and the tears are running salty into my mouth. I went to Allerton by myself and urged him to come back for all the right reasons. I rode on the motorcycle with him and I even learned a little bit about driving it. I made a tourniquet and stopped the bleeding. I did all of that.

Isn't that enough? Haven't I done enough? Do I really expect myself to do more? The voice wants in and so does the panic. The voice wanted to be the eye and now it wants in.

But the point is, I have done the rest of it, and now I can do this. Dr. Rowe tells me over and over that I can take control of my own life.

If I don't do this, Luke will die. I have done the rest, and I can do this.

I wipe my tears roughly on the jacket sleeve.

I yank with all my strength and kick down with all my might. Luke is grunting his pain. There is suddenly anger in me and only anger, adrenalin pumping through me like a fountain. I am angry at fear and loneliness. I am angry at suffering and paralysis. I am angry at disorientation and panic. I am furious at the scum who taunted me and molested me.

The throttle is right and the gearshift is left. The front brake is the right handbrake and the rear brake is the right foot pedal. You shift with your left toe and be sure you don't rest your leg against the tailpipe.

Once again I kick down with all my strength and the motor suddenly turns over and blubbers to life. I rev its throttle several times and ease it carefully into gear. We are in motion the way Luke taught me. I am doing this.

We are moving fast enough to keep balanced but I have to work my way carefully across the gravel surface until we pass through the wide-open gate.

I am gulping air; my gear shifting is clumsy but we gather speed. Faster, and even faster. The turns are scary, but I remember the way to the highway. The anger is still in me, and I *will* do this.

Luke holds on tight; it means he is still conscious. My father loved me. The road whizzes underneath and the cold wind whips my face and hair. The Iron Horse has a full tank of gas. The road is straight ahead.

Epilogue

11/4

I didn't win a prize at the science fair. Some of the exhibits were so sophisticated you would have thought only a professor could make them. It doesn't matter. I had a wonderful time with Miss Braverman and DeeDee, and I got to know a boy named Bryan. He's a nerd, but I'm sure I could use a good nerd in my life.

11/6

I had to stay after school today in Mr. MacFarlane's office to talk about the people who molested me. It was real scary naming names. My mother was there and also a policeman who took a lot of notes. Mr. MacFarlane had a long letter from Dr. Rowe, although I didn't see it.

I don't know what the consequences will be for DeWayne and Butch and Brenda. They will probably be suspended or even expelled. I don't dare think about the consequences for me, it's much too scary. I only hope I'll be able to sleep tonight. The next time I see Dr. Rowe I'll tell her all about this. She usually makes me feel better when I'm real scared.

11/8

My mother and I talked to Dr. Rowe today. We talked about my escapade on the road with Luke and how it was a bad decision because it was so desperate. But Dr. Rowe said at least I acted, now I have to learn about actions and decisions that are appropriate.

I'm supposed to see Dr. Rowe on Saturday mornings. Sometimes when I see Dr. Rowe, Mother is going to go with me. Mother is brand-new at therapy and she's not comfortable with it yet. We are supposed to try to figure out how the dynamics of an intense father and a withdrawn mother helped make me the way I am today. At least Mother and I will be working on it together.

I know I'll never be a cool person, but with the right medicine and my mother, I believe I can make it. I hope to have DeeDee and Luke in my life; friends make a difference. I can learn control and I can have a future. Dr. Rowe tells me so, and I trust her.

11/13

Today, I talked to Luke on the phone. He is back at Clark House, on the strictest probation there is. There's a name for it, which I can't remember. Sometime soon he's going to have a bench trial, which means a judge but no jury.

He has decided to go back to school. One reason he's allowed to do it is that Dr. Rowe wrote a supportive letter to the authorities. When we were talking on the phone, he told me I was right; Dr. Rowe is no bullshitter.

When he goes to school, he will be taken and picked up by a parole officer, but we will get to walk together in the halls. He still has stitches and a leg bandage, so we will walk slow. But that will be good for me; I always walk much too fast and keep my eyes down. I don't know if we will hold hands or not — I've never held a boy's hand and certainly not in public. It will feel secure being by his side. I wonder if Dr. Rowe would think that's a good way for me to think.

Who knows? Luke did tell me it's okay for me to come over to Clark House sometimes and help him with his homework.

195

11/15

DeeDee came over and we spent most of the day working on the pitiful Russian olive tree. I'm not sure why I wanted to, it must be important somehow. She gave all of the advice and did as much work as I did. We pruned and pruned. DeeDee says the fall is a good time to try to resuscitate a sickly tree. She had her uncle's deep-root feeder so we watered it and fertilized it down deep. It was hard to do it at what she called the tree's drip line, because of the concrete and gravel and blacktop, but we did our best and she has some hope for the tree. We got some occasional grief from some of the Surlies in the parking lot, but we mostly just ignored it.

At night, I had a dream that a mourning dove landed in the tree and cooed at me on my balcony, ever so peacefully. I'm not sure if the dream has a meaning, but I'll ask Dr. Rowe about it.

11/18

After school today, I picked up some trash and litter from around our building. There was some jeering, which made me shaky, but I wasn't about to get scrambled, and I got a full bag.

It was warm before supper, so I sat on the balcony to read. I have taken down the blankets and towels from the railing; I can see my tree better that way. One day there may actually be a mourning dove perched in it, who knows?

The book I am reading is called On the Road, by someone called Jack Kerouac. Luke gave it to me. It's not my type of book, but Luke says it's a classic, and maybe we'll be able to discuss it together. It's a book, I think, which a lot of people read in the fifties, then basically vanished. Some day I may tell him what a classic really is. His feelings won't be hurt. He'll just tell me what a good mind I have. He has a good mind too, but he doesn't realize it.

11/22

I have decided to spray paint the Beast. Mother and I are going to the mall today; I need to find a color which is an exact match with the rest of the sculpture. I reread the Beauty and the Beast story and the point is, the Beast is not really ugly at all, he only appears *to be.*

The most important thing about the spray painting is that I'm sure my dad didn't get the sculpture finished. He would have wanted it this way. I don't hear his voice anymore, but when I'm finishing the sculpture, I pray that somehow he will be hearing mine.